Bread In The Oven

BABY BREEDER SESSION 2

NATALIE ARTHUR

Cover Design by **Bookin' it Designs**

Formatting by **Natalie Arthur**

Bread In The Oven is part of the Baby Breeder Session 2 Series, but it includes characters from my Mancini Legacy series and my Cimaruta MC Chicago Series. All my books are all stand alone with NO cheating and HEA.

Even though they are standalone, they are best enjoyed if read in order.

Acknowledgments

Jessica, you are summer and I am winter. Always.

JD, thank you for spending late nights with and making sure I listened even when I didn't want to. Love you.

Kristen, we can do this. Together.

Nicole, I'm forever grateful that you're in my life.

Carissa, thank you for everything you do.

Danni, this journey is so crazy! Thank you for being here with me!

Tammy thank you for everything. For loving my books and supporting me.

Arthur, you've always supported me no matter how crazy my ideas are. I love you so much.

Mom, you've always been my biggest supporter and I don't know where I'd be without you.

Caoimhe-Lea, you drive me absolutely fucking crazy. But I wouldn't have it any other way. Love you.

Taye, Mary and everyone I'm forgetting who has supported my crazy ideas and continue to be with me, thank you. I truly couldn't do this without all of you.

Information

No part of this book or graphics were made with AI.
HUMAN CREATION ONLY

Bread In The Oven has NO cheating and a guaranteed HEA. It's part of the Baby Breeder Session 2 Series. And is connected to my Mancini Legacy Series and my Cimaruta MC Chicago Series.

Check out my website for current news and trigger warnings.
Mancini Legacy and Cimaruta MC family trees.
Nataliearthurbooks.com

Mancini Legacy and Cimaruta MC Dictionary

Cage - Motorized vehicle with four wheels. (Cars)

Chicago Panthers - Professional baseball team.

Chicago Redhawks - Professional hockey team.

Cimaruta MC, Chicago - Chicago Motorcycle club, Mother charter

Cut - Vest that patched in members of the MC wear to identify who they are and their rank.

Lake Renegade Township - Town owned by the Mancini family.

Lucciola Island - 'Firefly' Island, owned by the Mancini family and located in Massachusetts.

Lucciola Memorial Hospital - Hospital in Lake Renegade Township.

Mancini Grill - 5-star restaurant located inside the Legacy Hotel.

Rockers - Top rocker has the club's name on it, the bottom rocker has the club's location.

Sprite Lake Village - Town in Illinois, owned by the Laurent family.

The Legacy Hotel - Hotel in downtown Chicago owned by the Mancini family.

Galway - Town in Ireland.

ITALIAN

Amore - Love.

Coglione - Asshole.

Colomba mia - My dove.

Cugino - Cousin.

Cuore mio - My heart.

Dolcezza - Sweetness.

Farfalla - Butterfly.

Famiglia - Family.

Figlio - Son.

Fratello - Brother.

Fratellino - Baby brother.

Il mio mondo - My world.

Il mio pinguino - My penguin.

Mai Andato - Never Gone.

Mi dispiace - I'm sorry.

Mi passerotta - My little sparrow.

Nonno - Grandfather.

Nonna - Grandmother.

Ti abbiamo aspettato - We waited for you.

Ti voglio bene - I love you.

Zio - Uncle.

Zia - Aunt.

IRISH

Aintín - Aunty

Is í Gàidhlig ár gcéad teanga - Gaelic is our first language.

M'anam - My soul

Mo stór - My treasure.

FRENCH

D'accord petite sœur - Okay little sister

Je t'aime et Lorenzo - I love you and Lorenzo

Je t'aime - I love you

Je vous aime tous les deux - I love you both

Princesse - Princess

Toujours - Always

Toujours mes frères - Always my brothers

Tu es ma princesse - You are my princess

FAUSTO & LUNA
GRANDPARENTS
GIACOMO
SON
CAITRÍONA
DAUGHTER IN LAW
CELESTINO
GRANDSON
FRANCESCO
GRANDSON
SAOIRSE
GREAT GRANDDAUGHTER
ISABELLA
GRANDDAUGHTER
LUCIANA
GRANDDAUGHTER
GRAYSON
GREAT GRANDSON
BASTIANINI
FAMILY

KEARNEY FAMILY

Liam & Orfhlaith
GRANDPARENTS

Caitríona
DAUGHTER

Giacomo
SON IN LAW

Celestino
GRANDSON

Francesco
GRANDSON

Saoirse
GREAT GRANDDAUGHTER

Isabella
GRANDDAUGHTER

Luciana
GRANDDAUGHTER

Grayson
GREAT GRANDSON

MANCINI FAMILY

Pietro & Alessia
Grandparents

Enea (T)
Son

Antonio (T)
Son

Leonardo (T)
Son

Gráinne
Daughter-in-law

Rosaura
Daughter-in-law

Sebastiano*
Grandson

Salvatore^
Grandson

Domenico*
Grandson

Fiorella^
Granddaughter

Lorenzo+
Grandson

Gianluca^
Grandson

Giovanna+
Granddaughter

Rowan
Great Grandson

(T) = Triplets
* = Twins
+ = Twins
^ = Triplets

O'Connor
FAMILY

LIAM & RIOGHNACH
GRANDPARENTS

AIDEN
SON

ÉLODIE
DAUGHTER=IN LAW

EMMERSON

ELIAS

EASTON *

EZRA *

EDEN

GRANDKIDS

GRÁINNE
DAUGHTER

ENEA
SON-IN-LAW

SEBASTIANO *

DOMENICO *

LORENZO *

GIOVANNA *

GRANDKIDS

TWINS *

Cimaruta MC

President - Giacomo 'Forza' Bastianini

Vice President - Celestino 'Giustizia' Bastianini

Sgt-At-Arms - Francesco 'Bestia' Bastianini

Treasurer - Luciana 'Fuoco' Bastianini

Secretary - Isabella 'Dolce' Bastianini

Historian - Caitríona 'Forte' Bastianini

Road Captain - Connor 'Azrael' Byrne

Chaplain - Brennan 'Raziel' Doyle

Enforcer - Liam 'Amante' Murphy

Enforcer - Valentino 'Ombra' Marconi

Enforcer - Romana 'Fantasma' Vietti

Enforcer - Mitchell 'Granchio' Harris

Enforcer - Hollis 'Cavallo' Taylor

Enforcer - Rónán 'Ghiaccio' O'Callaghan

Enforcer - Fintan 'Toro' O'Callaghan

Prospect - Anthony Grimes

GIACOMO
CAITRÍONA
CELESTINO
ISABELLA
FRANCESCO
LUCIANA
MAEVE
RÓNÁN
SAOIRSE
GRAYSON
BASTIANINI
FAMILY

MANCINI FAMILY

Athanasiou
(Polar Bear shifters)

Zeus & Athena

Ares
Eros
Adonis
Apollo
Artemis

*Ares, Eros and Adonis are triplets
**Apollo and Artemis are twins

NIKOLAIDIS
(WHITE TIGER SHIFTERS)

Panagiotis & Stella

Georgios

Kostas

Calliope

*TRIPLETS

Contents

Bread In The Oven

Chapter One

Romano

When I made the decision to come to Chicago, it wasn't an easy one. I had suffered a huge loss, one that I still haven't been able to get past. I needed to get away from all the memories. Maybe it was a cowardly move to leave. Rome is my home, where I spent my whole life. But I had to. Everywhere I looked, I saw my wife and kids.

Since the day I met Amara in *scuola media superiore*, which is the equivalent of high school in the US, I never wanted anyone else. We were fourteen, and it was the first week of school. I saw her walk across the yard to a class we shared. It took me a few months to even get her to talk to me. But I finally got her to not only talk to me, but she agreed to go to the movies with me. I felt like the luckiest guy in school.

After our movie night, we spent every moment we could together. In Italy, the first two years of secondary education are mandatory. The last three are voluntary. Amara and I decided we wanted to continue going to school. I decided to learn how to fix motorcycles and cars. Amara wanted to be a teacher.

We were eighteen when we found out we were pregnant with Bruno. Romeo was born two years later and we rounded out our family with baby Oriana two years after that. We had talked about having more babies, and I found out that she was three months pregnant when the accident happened. The guy that killed my family got off easy—he died that day too. I never got to have revenge on him and I never will.

The family Amara and I had created together was gone in the blink of an eye. All it took was one person's bad judgement to take away everything that I held in my heart. I wasn't with them when the accident happened and that kills me every day. I usually drove them everywhere, but that day I had things to do for my MC. I've been a patched member of the Silenziatori Motorcycle Club in Rome, Italy for eleven years. My job with them was being an enforcer.

The day of the accident, my oldest son, Bruno, was seven. He had a football game and I planned on meeting them there. They never made it to the game. And my heart has never been the same. I had to leave my home and start over. The memories were just too much.

Luckily, I had options. I was able to transfer from my original MC to our mother club, Cimaruta MC in Chicago. Since being here, I feel like this is where I'm meant to be. I still miss my family every day, but at least now I'm not reminded of them everywhere I look.

When I first transferred, I slipped easily into the role of enforcer. It's what I did for my old MC. But now I'm also a bodyguard for Maeve. She's the wife of Francesco 'Bestia' Bastianini, the sergeant-at-arms. Every woman in the family has a bodyguard. My situation is a little different than other bodyguards. I don't live with Francesco and Maeve, and I usually only accompany her when Francesco can't. Or if he needs extra back up. The rest of the time, I do whatever my president, Giacomo 'Forza' Bastianini asks of me.

Our club is also different from most motorcycle

clubs. Our main council is made up of the Bastianini family, including the women. When I first heard about our mother club doing this, I thought it was a crazy idea. But now being here and getting to know Caitríona 'Forte' Bastianini and her daughters, Isabella 'Dolce' and Luciana 'Fuoco' Bastianini, I like how it's done. The Bastianini family have taken me in as one of their own and have given me a new family.

But being a part of a new family doesn't take away the pain of losing my own family. I haven't told anyone about what happened. All the club knows is that I needed a new start. I know they all know something happened that made me leave, but they respect the fact that I will tell them when I'm ready.

Simone

My parents have never allowed me to do anything. I've never gone to a real school, I've never played sports. And I've never had any friends besides my siblings. There are four of us: my older brother Thomas, me, Robin and the baby, Lucy. We are all two years apart. When Thomas turned twenty-two last year, he left and took Robin with him. They wanted me to go too, but I couldn't leave Lucy here alone. So I stayed with her.

We do get to go out. Once in a while we get to go grocery shopping with our mother. That's how I know what's out there, and how Thomas got the idea to leave. He tried to wait till Lucy was eighteen, but something happened and he changed his plans. He said he had to leave then.

The one thing my mother taught me was how to cook and bake. When I turned sixteen, she started making me cook dinner. I had to make the main meal and dessert every night. Plus, I still had to keep up with my studies. It was challenging, but I learned to get it all done.

When I promised Lucy I wouldn't leave her, I thought I could handle another two years of being here. But lately I'm questioning that. My father had never been an abusive man, but since Thomas left? He's been yelling at us a lot. And he's started hitting me. My mother doesn't do anything about it. She just sits and watches. Or she'll leave the room. When he gets mad, it's usually for no good reason. A pillow left crooked on our bed, or I forgot to put the place settings 'just right.'

I need to leave, but Lucy is only seventeen.

"You need to get out of here. Like Thomas and

Robin. Do you think you can find them?" Lucy whispers as we lie in our beds.

"They told me where they were going. But I don't know if they're still there. And I can't leave you here alone with them." I frown.

"Yes you can. I can do this, but you have to promise to come back for me."

"I won't leave you," I say again. "We'll go together."

Now I have to figure out when we can leave. When Thomas and Robin left, my parents put alarms on the doors and windows. They set it anytime they leave the house and while we sleep. During the day, my mother watches our every move. Except when we go to the bathroom. That's the only time we're allowed alone time. And I know that taking Lucy with me is dangerous because she's not eighteen yet. But I have to, I don't think we'll survive another year.

I will find a way to get us out of here. I can get a job somewhere, I don't know how but I know I can. I can cook, clean and bake. I wish I knew where Thomas and Robin were so we could be with them. A part of me is afraid to do this with just me and Lucy, yet I know this is what we need to do.

Lucy and I have been planning for a month now. I don't know where we'll go yet but I think we'll head north. When I was younger, I heard my father say he and my mother were from Missouri. That's south of us and I don't want to take the chance that we could run into any of their families. Even though we've never met any of them.

The plan that Lucy and I came up with is that we will get out the front door. The alarm will go off, but I know where we can hide until it's safe. I'm so darn scared. I don't know what my parents will do if they catch us. But I can do this, for me and for Lucy.

Then we'll head north, I'm not sure how far north. But I know the busses are cheap and before Thomas left, he gave me one thousand dollars and told me to keep it safe. That it was the money I would need to leave. I asked him where he got it, and he told me not to worry about it. I miss him and Robin so much. All he said was he was going to go north, maybe we'll get lucky and find them.

Chapter Two

Simone

Tomorrow night is when we're going to leave. Part of me is scared because I'm leaving everything I know behind. But there's that voice inside that's saying my father is only going to get worse. I think when he lost control over Thomas, he just snapped. And if I leave Lucy behind, I know he'll start hitting her. I can't stand that thought.

"Do you have everything you need?" I whisper to Lucy.

We've been quietly packing a backpack for each of us. Just clothes and a few things we've had since we were little. For me it's a stuffed cow that

Thomas gave me when I was five. I also made sure to take the one picture I have of the four of us. My mother took it before Thomas left. I make sure I have the money in my bag. And just a few changes of clothes.

"I think so," she says.

"Remember if we get separated for any reason, we meet at the bus station. Thomas said the bus is the cheapest way for us to leave."

"I remember," she says. "Hey, Simone?"

"Yeah?"

"Are you scared?"

I look at my baby sister, then reach out to hug her.

"I am scared. But we can do this, and we have each other. So it makes me less scared."

Lucy nods as she hugs me. "Why are mom and dad like this? Why did they have us if they didn't want us?"

I sigh. "I don't think that's what happened. I do think they wanted us, but maybe something happened and they changed."

She thinks about that for a minute. "Yeah, I hope so. It would be really sad if they didn't want us from the start."

"I agree. But I'm glad you're here, life wouldn't be the same without you."

Lucy smiles at me. "I feel the same way. And thank you for not leaving me behind. I love you, Simone."

"I love you too, Lucy. Thomas and Robin love us, I know it. I just wish I knew what happened to make him change his mind about leaving. Because I know it was really hard for him to leave us behind."

"Maybe we'll find them and we'll get to ask him. Because you're right, Thomas would never have left us. Something happened and he had to. Just like we have to now."

"Tomorrow night we will be free from all of this. And we'll make a better life for us."

I wish I could promise her that. But I can't. All I can do is my best to protect my baby sister.

The next morning we try to act like it's any other day. It's not as easy as you would think. We have to do everything the same as we always do. Lucy keeps telling me how nervous she is and that it feels like our mother knows something is going on. I keep telling her she can't know, and that she has to try and relax. Or she will figure something out. Or our father will when he gets home from work.

The whole day goes a lot smoother than I thought it would. Lucy did her school work and my mother had me cook beef stew and make an apple cobbler for dinner. I hope that wherever we decide to stop, I can get a job cooking or baking.

The plan is to wait till our parents go to bed. Then sneak down and leave through the front door. The alarm will go off, but as long as we move fast, we can make it to the neighbor's wall. And hope that our parents go the opposite way. But just in case, we will keep moving. While we take our showers, we will finish packing our backpacks. That's all we can afford to take is what we can stuff in there.

Our bathroom is connected to our room. It's making it easier for us to get our stuff together. Tonight I get to shower first. I make sure I grab a weeks worth of underwear and socks, rolling them as small as I can so I can get more in. I take two pairs of jeans and four shirts. I'll wear another pair of jeans and shirt with my jacket when we leave. I'll pack my toothbrush right before we leave.

We decided we're not taking any shampoos or body wash. We can buy things like that when we get to where we will stay for the first night. I'm so nervous as I grab my clothes to pack, moving as fast as I can. I don't want to forget anything that I need. I wish there were more things that I wanted to keep to remember living here and our family. But there's nothing in this house that I want to remember. I did manage to find Lucy's birth certificate, and mine too. Last month when our parents went out, I looked around and they were in a box in their closet. So far, I don't think they've noticed they're missing. There were multiple copies and I only took one of each. I also grabbed Thomas' and Robin's. Maybe there's hope we'll still find them.

After my shower, I hide my backpack in our closet. Lucy goes to take her shower and pack her bag. I check to make sure I grabbed the picture of my siblings and me.. Before Thomas and Robin left. Even though I never want to see my parents again, I want to remember my brother and sister.

Our parents go to bed around the same time every night. Their room is at the opposite end of the hallway from ours. We hear them come upstairs and close their bedroom door. I look at the clock and it reads ten forty-five. We agreed we would wait for thirty minutes after they go to bed. I need to make sure that they're sleeping.

Those thirty minutes feels like forever, but it's finally eleven fifteen. I look over at Lucy and she's staring back at me.

"Are you sure this is what you want?" I whisper to her.

She nods at me. "I can't be here without you. And watching Father hit you? That's something I can't do anymore."

I get up slowly and as quietly as I can, making sure Lucy is right behind me. I know for a fact that the alarm won't go off until I open the door. So we need to make it to the front door and be ready to run as soon as I get that door open. We should have at least a minute to run before my parents can get to the front door. I grab Lucy's hand and squeeze it before I open our bedroom door. I feel her squeeze mine back. It's time to go.

We get downstairs and to the front door. I take a deep breath and make sure Lucy is close enough to get out before me. I will be the one to close the door. One more deep breath and I twist the bolt lock on the door. I look at Lucy and she nods.

I grab the door handle and twist it, yanking the door open. It takes a second before the alarms starts blaring. Before it does, Lucy is out the door and running. I pull the door closed behind me as I run behind her. We stick to the trees and shadows in case our parents look out any of the windows that's facing out the front of the house.

We don't stop running until we get to the bus stop. I knew which direction the bus stop was from our house. I would keep track of the street names when we would go out with our parents. Luckily, the bus comes right when we get there.

"Does this bus go to the main station?" I ask the driver.

"The main station is my last stop. It'll take about fifteen minutes," the bus driver answers me.

I thank the driver and pay for Lucy and me. We grab a seat and huddle close.

"We're going to be okay," I whisper to Lucy, she's shaking as I hold her.

"I know, I'll always be okay as long as I'm with you." She sniffles.

The fifteen minutes it takes to get to the main bus station seems to go by really slow. I keep wishing it would hurry up. As we get off the bus, I thank the driver again. She smiles at us, but she has a sad look in her eyes. It's like she knows we're running away from something. I just hope she doesn't call the police or tell anyone about us.

Romano

Lake Renegade Township was founded by Pietro Bastianini and Liam Kearney. They came from Italy and Ireland to give their children a better life. When Giacomo was voted in as president, both Pietro and Liam went back to their home countries and started chapters there. They've since stepped down from those MC's, but they are still an important part of our clubs.

Lake Renegade is very different than Rome. But I've come to love the small town and the slower lifestyle. Every morning, I get on my bike and ride from one end of our township to the other. It's soothing to my soul to ride. Amara loved to ride on my bike with me. No one's ever been on the back of my bike except her. And I don't think anyone else ever will be again.

I now spend my days making sure Maeve is safe when she's out. On my days off, I explore the campgrounds. It borders all three properties, owned by the Bastianini, Mancini, Athanasiou and

Nikolaidis families. The Athanasiou and Nikolaidis families are new, they moved here from Greece about six months ago. And recently, we found out that they are shifters. Yes, real shifters. The Athanasiou clan are polar bear shifters and the Nikolaidis clan are white tigers. Before meeting them, shifters were part of fantasies and made-up stories. Knowing they're real is still such a crazy concept.

In the campgrounds, there are two mountains and an assortment of lakes and rivers. It's a beautiful place and I wish Amara and the kids could've seen it. There are also otters on the Bastianini property. That started at the Cimaruta chapter club in Galway, Ireland. When Francesco brought his woman and their daughter to Chicago, he wanted to give Saoirse the otters. So we all took classes to learn about otters and what they eat and how to take care of them. And every six months, we have a veterinarian come out and make sure they're thriving. We have seven of them now. We're also registered as an otter sanctuary.

Chapter Three

Simone

We did it. We got away and we're on the bus to a town called Lake Renegade. Lucy thought it sounded like a town that would protect us. Who am I to disagree? The bus ride is going to take about four hours so I told Lucy to get some rest. I know I won't be sleeping till we get off the bus. I'm still a little scared that our parents are following us.

It's hard to see out the windows of the bus because it's dark out. But they've dimmed the lights so people can sleep. From what I can see, it's all farmland. I wonder if it would've been a better idea to be in one of these smaller towns? But we're still too close to where we were, and I want to put more distance between us.

Four hours later, we're getting off the bus. My first impression of Lake Renegade Township is that it feels right. I don't know how to really explain it. But I feel like we're home.

"It feels good here," Lucy whispers to me.

I put my arm around her. "I think we found our home. Let's find a motel so we can get a room."

We walk about five minutes from the bus station and see a motel called Lakeside Hideaway. It doesn't look too scary so we head inside. There's an older lady with a kind smile at the counter.

"Morning, girls. How can I help you?' she asks.

"We need a room, is it possible to get one with two beds, please?"

"Of course. How long will you be staying with us?"

"Um, well I don't know yet, do we have to have a check out date?" I ask. That makes me a little nervous.

"Oh no, you can stay as long as you need. I have the perfect room for you. It's right by the elevator and the ice machine. It also has a kitchenette, so you can make your own food if you want."

"Thank you so much, we really appreciate that."

"If you have any problems, or need anything, you call the front desk and we'll be happy to help. There's someone here twenty-four hours a day," she says to us as she hands me two little envelopes. "One key card for each of you."

I take them from her and give one to Lucy.

"Take the elevator on the left and you're on the sixth floor. Room six-oh-one."

"Thank you so much," I say as we turn to find our room.

The room she gave us is bigger than the room we shared back home. It's a corner room so there's a big window in the living room. It overlooks the town. In the living room there's a couch, which sits next to the kitchenette. Then there's the bedroom, with another huge window. This one faces the mountains, they're so beautiful. It also has two huge beds. And the bathroom? It has a tub! Lucy is going back and forth looking out the windows and giggling. I've never seen her so happy.

Now that we're here and we have a temporary home, it's time for me to find a job. I go over to the living room window to look at our new home. It's a pretty town, and from where I'm standing, I can see a bakery. It's called Precious Risings Bakery and that's the first place I'm going to go to. That would be a dream to work at a bakery.

"Did you want to come with me to walk around? I want to stop in that bakery over there and see if they're hiring," I say to Lucy.

"Is it okay if I stay here? I'll go with you later to find food?"

"Sure, I'll be back soon. Don't open the door for anyone," I say to her as she nods.

"I promise."

I grab my purse and my room key and head out. I walk straight over to the bakery and there's a 'help wanted' sign in the window. That has to be a sign that we've done the right thing...right?

I open the door and head inside. It smells heavenly in here—cinnamon, frosting and all kinds of sweets.

"Hi! What can I get you today?" a woman asks as she smiles at me.

"Hi, I was wondering about the 'help wanted' sign."

"Are you interested in applying? Have you worked in a bakery before?"

"I am interested. And no, I've never worked in a bakery. But I do know how to bake."

The woman smiles at me. "I tell you what, I'll give you a shot. You come in tomorrow morning at three am. That's when we start prepping and baking for the day."

"Really? Thank you so much! I'd like to buy a few of your goodies too. Can I get a chocolate chip muffin and a strawberry shortcake?"

"Of course," she says. "By the way, my name is Rosaura Mancini. I'm one of the owners."

She hands me my box of pastries.

"I'm Simone. My sister and I just moved here."

"Welcome to Lake Renegade. I hope you like it here."

"We love it so far. How much do I owe you?"

"Nothing, that's on me. I look forward to seeing you in the morning."

"Are you sure?"

My parents always said no one gives anything to you for nothing.

"I'm positive. Where are you staying?"

"We're staying at the Lakeside Hideaway."

She smiles again. "You let me know if you have any problems. Here's my card, it has my number on it if you need anything."

"Thank you so much. I'll see you at three!"

I walk out of the bakery. I can't believe how nice Rosaura was. And I have a job! My first job, I'm so excited. I hear loud rumblings and I look up to see a few motorcycles riding down the street. I watch them as I cross the intersection. They're all wearing vests and in the back it says Cimaruta MC Chicago. One is watching me as they head into the bakery. I don't know why but all of a sudden I feel the need to know who he is. I must be going crazy.

When I get back to our room, Lucy is looking out the window still.

"Did you see those guys on the motorcycles? That was so cool!"

I laugh. "I did see them, their bikes are so loud."

I show her the goodies I brought and we share both of them.

"I start working at the bakery at three am. The owner is the one that hired me. Her name is Rosaura Mancini."

Lucy shrieks, "That's so awesome, Simone! I knew this place was going to be perfect."

"I still want to figure out how you can finish high school. Maybe we can see about you taking your GED. Or maybe we can enroll you in the high school here. We could say we don't have any documents because it got lost or burned in a fire? I don't know. But I know I want you to finish."

I do have our birth certificates, but I don't know if they can track us with that. We decided to tell everyone that our parents died and I'm the legal guardian of her. But I'm pretty sure I need legal papers for that. All I can do is say that those papers are coming. That it just happened.

"I know and I want to finish too. But I don't want them to find us either."

I sigh. That's the biggest obstacle to all of this. I'm hoping that I can ask Rosaura if she can pay me in cash. I learned about some things from when our parents let us watch TV. It wasn't often, but there were some shows we got to watch. I don't remember which one it was, but I do remember seeing that. Being paid in cash means your name isn't on any paperwork.

Maybe one day we'll be able to tell someone about what happened to us. I also still hope we can find Thomas and Robin.

Romano

Some days, my club brothers head into town and get some of the best pastries in Illinois. The bakery is owned by the Mancini and Bastianini wives. Today while we were headed to the bakery, I saw a woman who made my head turn. That hasn't happened since Amara and I never expected to look at another woman again. But watching her walk across the street in front of us? Damn. I want to know who she is and where she's from.

"You okay, Fantasma?" My VP, Celestino 'Giustizia' Bastianini, asks.

"Yeah, all good. Need pastries." I chuckle.

"Mam said they made that strawberry shortcake you love."

"Your mam is the best." I smile, taking a quick look for the beauty I saw. I spot her going into the Lakeside Hideaway. I make a mental note to go over there after I get my strawberry shortcake.

"Hi Rosaura," Celestino says.

"Hey, guys." She smiles as she hands me my shortcake and a donut for Celestino.

Caitríona comes out from the back and comes over to give us a hug.

"Did you see that pretty girl that just left the bakery?" she asks as she sits with us.

"Who was she?" Celestino asks.

"Stop talking with food in your mouth." His mam frowns at him.

Celestino grins at her. "Sorry, Mam."

"We just hired her, she said her name was Simone. And she seemed like she was running from something. I need your brother to look into her. Just to be safe."

Francesco takes care of our security and is the one we go to for anything tech related. Celestino gets his phone out and texts his twin.

"He said he's on it," Celestino says.

"Thank you, son." She smiles and kisses his forehead.

Celestino grins at his mam, you can see the love they have for each other. All the kids have respect and love for their parents. Even the little ones have it, there's not a lot of back talk or sassing in any of the families. I see a lot of kids doing the opposite when we're out. I don't know how those parents deal with kids who talk back or sass them. Hell, even now if I talked to my parents that way? My mother wouldn't hesitate to smack me.

While we're eating our pastries, Caitríona tells us her feelings about Simone. She thinks she's not only running, but that there's more to what she's going through. Rosaura didn't want to ask her too many questions yet. She didn't want to scare her off.

If Simone is running from something, I'm glad she landed in Lake Renegade. We will all make sure she's taken care of. And if we find out someones hurt her, well I'm going to have a serious talk with whoever did it.

Chapter Four

Romano

Today is Simone's first day here at the bakery. And luck has it that Francesco was planning on staying with Maeve today. So I told Caitríona that I would come to the bakery with her and her bodyguard, Connor 'Azrael' Byrne. Our women never go anywhere alone, same with the Mancini women. Gráinne and Rosaura Mancini, the other two owners of Precious Risings Bakery are the wives of Enea and Leonardo Mancini. Enea is the head of the Chicago mafia and Leonardo is his consigliere. They have a triplet brother, Antonio, who oversees all the businesses.

"You need pastries this early in the morning?" Azrael asks me.

"Don't we all?" I laugh.

Azrael keeps staring at me. Okay, I don't usually go to the bakery this early. Nosy bastard.

"Okay, I'm ready to go. Gráinne and Rosaura should be there already. We have a wedding to get prepped for. And we're training our new baker today," Caitríona tells us.

I try not to grin too much, but I can't help it. Just the mention of Simone makes me smile. I never thought my heart would want to get to know someone again. But here I am thinking about a woman that I saw crossing the street. Amara and I had talked about it, what we would do if one of us was lost. She told me that she would want me to be happy and find love again. I told her I want her to love me forever and no one else. Okay, I was joking...kind of. But truthfully, I would want Amara to be happy if I was the one that was gone.

We get into one of the cages we own and head to the bakery. Again, my smile comes out as I see Simone waiting outside the front door. She's early.

"Hi! Morning! I was so excited I couldn't wait to start." She smiles as she sees Caitríona.

We all smile at her. She's fucking adorable.

"Morning, Simone. This is Connor and

Romano, you'll be seeing Connor here every day. Romano comes by a lot, but this morning he wanted pastries." She chuckles.

"It's nice to meet you both." Simone smiles and shakes Connors hand, then takes mine. I swear when I touch her hand I hear a voice say she's mine.

"Morning," Connor says as he shakes her hand.

"Morning," I say as I hold her hand. She's not trying to take her hand back and I'm pretty sure everyone is staring at us.

"We should head inside," Caitríona says as she gives me a look that tells me she knows something's up.

I look at her and try to keep my face neutral. But if there's one thing I know about Caitríona, she knows all of us really well. She knows when we're covering shit up. Even though it hasn't been that long for me? She knows me, and sometimes that's a little scary. Simone gets to work with Gráinne after meeting Arturo and Seamus, their bodyguards. Caitríona comes over to me.

"You like our new baker," she says. She's telling me, not asking me.

I look at her and sigh.

"There's something about her. But she's looks so young, how old is she?"

"She says she's twenty-one. I don't think she's lying, she didn't hesitate when I asked her."

I nod. So she's five years younger than me. That's not so bad, when I first saw her I thought she was maybe eighteen. I would never touch her if she were younger than that. I really hope she's not lying about her age. I will still protect her no matter what her age.

"What do you think she's running from?" I ask Caitríona quietly.

"I don't know. Maybe an abusive ex?"

I frown, that thought makes my blood boil.

"You do like her. That look right there is my confirmation." She smiles at me. "I know we said we'd never push you to tell us what happened to you back home. But know that whatever it is, we will always be here for you."

My head drops as I look at my hands. I think it's time to tell someone about what happened.

"I lost my family," I say softly.

Caitríona puts her hands over mine. "I'm so sorry, Romano. Can you tell me what happened?"

I take a breath and look into her eyes.

"My wife and three children were on their way to my oldest's football game. A driver came out of nowhere and hit them head on."

Caitríona gasps softly. She gets up and comes around to my side and hugs me.

"I was supposed to be there. And because I wasn't, I lost all of them. Amara was three months pregnant when it happened. Bruno was seven, Romeo was five and our baby, Oriana was three."

I pull my phone out and show her a picture of my family.

"They're beautiful, Romano. I can't even begin to know how you feel or what to say."

"There's nothing to say. My world died that day. And I tried to stay in Rome for my parents. But I just couldn't. They said they understood. So I put in my transfer to come here. And when Giacomo accepted it, I left my home to start new here."

"How long has it been?" she asks.

"Almost a year and a half."

Caitríona hugs me again. "Thank you for telling me, I won't tell anyone until you're ready to share. But I think that Amara would be happy if you found someone to love again. I know that if I was gone, I would want Giacomo to fall in love again. It's hard to imagine that. But I would never want him to suffer for the rest of his time here."

"Thank you. I appreciate that. Amara and I talked about the what ifs. And she said that to me.

That she wouldn't want me to be alone. I haven't even wanted to look at another woman until I saw Simone yesterday. Part of me feels like I'm betraying Amara. But I hear her voice telling me it's okay, that she wants me to be happy again."

Caitríona smiles. "It sounds like she's happy that you might have found someone."

I give her a small smile. "Thank you."

I look into the kitchen area and see Simone looking at Caitríona and me. I give her a smile and wave.

Simone

I can feel the heat rising in my cheeks when Romano smiles and waves at me. I've had butterflies in my stomach since I saw him yesterday. Now he's here and he's even more handsome up close. Rosaura and Gráinne are watching me and I start to giggle.

"You like Romano?" Gráinne smiles.

"He's very handsome," I say softly.

"He's a good guy. In fact, all the men in our families are good men. They will never hurt you and if you're in trouble? They'll all help you,"

Rosaura says.

I feel like they're trying to tell me something. Like they know I'm running from my parents. There's something about these three women that make me want to blab all my secrets. But there's still a tiny part of me that's saying 'what if it's a trap?' I tell them what's happened to me and Lucy...then they turn us in? Or worse, say that I kidnapped Lucy, since she's technically a minor. It makes me sad to know that I can never tell anyone our secrets.

"I want you to know that you're safe here. That you can trust us. All of us," Gráinne says to me. "We're all family here. And we take care of each other. If you need that, we're here for you."

I look into her eyes and see the sincerity in them. Against what I had originally planned, I find myself blurting out what we did. Gráinne and Rosaura stop what they're doing and sit down next to me.

"I had to get out of there, but I couldn't leave Lucy behind." My tears start falling on my hands as I stare at them.

Gráinne stands and embraces me. "You're safe now. You don't ever have to worry about being hurt by your parents again."

"You and Lucy are safe here. I promise you

that. Do you know where your brother and sister went?" Rosaura asks.

I shake my head no. "There was no way for Thomas to tell me where they went. And I don't know how to search for them. But I miss them everyday. If Lucy had been older, we would've all left together."

They both nod their heads in understanding.

"I wanted to wait until Lucy turned eighteen, but my father started hitting me. And I worried that if I left her, he would start to hit Lucy too. He never laid a hand on me before Thomas and Robin left."

They both hug me this time. I can't remember a time when I had two hugs in one day. Well, besides from my brother and sisters.

"Will you allow us to tell our families about you and Lucy?" Gráinne asks.

The thought of that scares me. What if they tell on us? Or they decide they don't want to help us like Gráinne and Rosaura want to?

"I can see you're scared. But I give you my word that there's no one in our families that would ever turn you away," Rosaura says.

I nod slowly. I already spilled everything to them, I can't take it back. So I guess I need to go forward and try to trust them.

"You stay here and keep prepping. We need to talk to Caitríona."

"Okay," I answer as I go back to prepping the dough for the flakey pastries.

I look up and see Romano watching me again. Gráinne and Rosaura are sitting with him and Caitríona at the table. I watch his features go from smiling to angry. Could he be angry at me? After what feels like forever, they all get up and head towards me. Suddenly I'm scared and I don't know why.

Romano walks straight to me and gathers me in his arms. He's huge and he towers over me, it's like being wrapped in a blanket. I'm also pretty sure his biceps are bigger than my head.

"I'm sorry your parents hurt you the way they did. But that's something you'll never have to worry about again. You and your sister have found a new home and a new family." He has the most beautiful Italian-accented voice. I've only ever heard a voice like his on TV.

I've never hugged a man before. Well my brother and once in a while my father. This hug feels different and it's making my emotions swirl around like a tornado.

"Thank you," I whisper. I can feel more tears

falling, Romano pulls back slightly and wipes them away.

"You're safe. Now when will we get to meet Lucy?" He smiles at me.

Chapter Five

Simone

I can't believe how lucky Lucy and I are. Yesterday we were running from our parents, and today? Today we found a town and a new family. I can't explain why I trust them, it *has* only been one day. But I do. I feel it in my soul. And then there's Romano. I feel like I know him, and I need to be with him. Now, I've never been with any man, and I'm sure Romano has been with other women. What if he doesn't want me?

The rest of my first day goes by faster than I want it to. I got to help with the baking and with selling what we baked. They also let me help make some of the wedding items. There's going to be a big wedding in two days. It's exciting to see everything they're doing for it. This is definitely my dream job. I've noticed that Romano has stayed within my eyeliner. And most times when I look over at him, he's looking at me too. There's a sadness in his eyes, though. Maybe one day he'll tell me his story.

Before I know it, my first official day is over. Rosaura asked if I could hang around for a bit. I will need to check on Lucy soon. I hope she's okay.

"Why don't you go get Lucy and come back?" Gráinne says to me. "We can all have dinner later if you'd like."

I smile. "That would be really great. Are you sure?"

"Yes. We would love to meet Lucy and for the two of you to join us. We can show you where we live and you can meet the rest of the families. I warn you, there's a lot of us. So don't worry about remembering everyone." She chuckles.

"Thank you so much. I'll go get Lucy and be right back."

"Take Romano with you. No one goes anywhere alone," Gráinne says.

I turn to look for Romano, and realize he's standing right next to me.

"Let's go get Lucy." He smiles at me.

He opens the door and I follow him out. I see him looking around and watching people around us. And at the same time, he's making sure I'm close to him. I feel safe when I'm with him, and that's an odd feeling for me. It's not that I felt unsafe with my parents. But I never felt like they were protecting us. It felt like they were keeping us hidden from the world.

We were allowed to go to a few places as a family. One consistent outing happened every Saturday evening—that was for church. And once a week to help do the grocery shopping. We had some of the other kids our age at church that we were able to talk to. But we knew better than to tell them how we lived. And when they would invite us over, we had to make up some excuse as to why we couldn't go. Eventually they stopped asking. We still talked to them at church, but they never asked us to come over for birthday parties or to hang out.

There was a boy at church, his name was Bryce. We got to hang out and talk in our youth group. As we were leaving our group one day, he asked me out and I thought my father was going to lose it. My father pulled me away so fast I didn't even have the chance to say anything. Then my father went over to Bryce and said something to him. That was the last time Bryce said anything to me. It made me sad that he stopped talking to me. We had fun talking, but because of whatever my father said to him, he stayed away from me in our group sessions too.

As we walk to Lakeside Hideaway, I keep looking around expecting to see my parents. I'm so afraid that they'll find us and force us to go back with them. I know I'm old enough to fight them. But Lucy isn't, she still has ten months before she'll turn eighteen.

"Are you okay?" Romano asks me. "You keep looking around like you're waiting for someone to pop up."

"I-I'm worried that my parents will find us," I say softly.

"Look at me, Simone. Even if your parents were to show up in Lake Renegade, they wouldn't be able to touch you or Lucy. I promise you that."

"But how can you promise that? Lucy isn't old enough yet. And I can't let her go back alone."

"I can promise that because I know me and I know what my family here is capable of."

I look into his eyes, they're blue and green and as I stare into them, it looks like they're changing colors. He wraps his arms around me again. And instantly I feel like nothing can hurt me or Lucy.

"Thank you," I whisper as I lay my head on his chest. I feel him kiss the top of my head and it makes my body tingle.

We get to the motel and head up to our room. I open the door and we see Lucy sitting on the couch watching TV. When she sees Romano, she jumps up and backs up.

"A-Are we in trouble?" she whispers as she starts crying.

I rush over to her and hold her.

"No, we're not in trouble. In fact, we're the luckiest girls around. This is Romano, he and his family are going to help us."

Romano

Watching the way Lucy reacted to seeing me is worriesome. She bolted off that couch so fast that she almost smacked into the wall. What the fuck did their parents do to them? I want to find them so that I can beat the fuck out of them. And put the fear of God in them like they did to my girl and her sister.

I stay where I am, I don't want to scare Lucy anymore than she already is. I'm a big guy and I probably scare people in general. But when you're running from being abused? That has to add an extra layer to the fear.

Lucy slowly makes her way over to me and puts her hand out to shake mine.

"It's nice to meet you, Romano."

I smile at her. "It's really great to meet you, Lucy. Simone has talked about you all day. Everyone's excited to meet you."

"Really?" she asks as a smile lights up her face. She has the same smile as my Simone.

Whoa. Where did that come from? 'My Simone'?

"Really. We should get back to the bakery. I think we're going to the Cimaruta property for dinner," I say to both of them.

"What's the Cimaruta property?" Simone asks.

I explain how the Mancinis, Bastianinis, Athanasious' and the Nikolaidis' share the property. And how there's ponds and rivers that they can swim in. Their eyes get huge as I'm describing all of it. I can't wait for them to actually see it. Hearing about it is one thing. Actually seeing it is another. I heard the stories before I came here, and my imagination was nothing compared to the reality.

"It sounds so wonderful." Lucy giggles.

I watch Simone as she watches her sister. The love in her eyes is unmistakable, I can see why she couldn't leave Lucy behind. Maybe we'll be able to help them find their brother and sister. I'll have to talk to Sebastiano, Francesco and Salvatore. Sebastiano and Francesco are our tech gurus and Salvatore is a detective with the Chicago Police. If anyone can find them, they can. I want to say this to Simone and Lucy, but at the same time, I don't want to get their hopes up yet.

We make our way back to the bakery, where everyone is waiting for us.

"This is my sister Lucy. Lucy, this is Caitríona, Rosaura, Gráinne, Connor, Arturo and Seamus."

Lucy shyly shakes each of their hands. Caitríona, Rosaura and Gráinne embrace her. You can see the surprise on Lucy's face, which transforms into the biggest smile. These girls are going to learn what it's like to truly have a family and to be loved. I can't stand the idea that a simple hug is something they're not used to. I'm determined to change that, we all are. I learned that when I moved here—the Mancinis and Bastianinis love to hug. A lot.

We head to the property, which takes about fifteen minutes. I have a feeling the women are going to ask Simone and Lucy to come live with us. I'm not opposed to that idea, in fact I think it's a damn good one. After all the introductions are made, the women take them inside to show them around.

A hand claps me on the back.

"So Caitríona tells me you like Simone," Giacomo 'Forza' Bastianini, my club president says.

I drop my head. "That didn't take long." I sigh.

"She looks like she's been really sheltered, I know you'll be careful. And you also know we will support whatever you both want."

I nod. "I know that. I don't know what she wants. Or hell what I want. I just know there's something telling me I have to be with her. I would never force her to do anything. I need to talk to her and make sure we want the same things. But I know she's innocent in so many ways. She told us her story and I want to find her parents and show them what happens to people like them."

"I'm not sure what you've been through, but we're glad you're here with us now."

"Thanks, Forza. I appreciate that a lot. I was lost for a long time, I don't even know what made me choose to come here. But I'm glad I did."

Chapter Six

Simone

There's so many people to meet when we get to the property. The one person that's always near me is Romano. No matter where I am, I can feel him nearby or watching me. And it doesn't make me feel uncomfortable, I feel like I need to be near him too. But then that little voice of doubt creeps in saying why would he want me?

I've been talking to Luciana Bastianini, Caitríona's youngest daughter. She's married to a guy named Rónán, who's almost as big as Romano. They have an adorable son, Grayson, who's a year old. And I've seen a few women walking around that she calls 'bunnies.' I'm not exactly sure what that means, but they don't seem to be family or to be with any of the men here. I saw one of them go over to Romano and touch his arm, then whisper in his ear. He shook his head 'no' and she didn't look very happy. I watched him walk away from her and that made me smile. I don't know why, but when she touched him, it made me angry.

"Does Romano have a girlfriend?" I ask Luciana.

"Nope. He's been with us for a year now and he's never been serious about anyone."

"Do you mean he's been with these women? Like more than one?"

That thought makes me angrier than watching that bunny touch his arm. Luciana looks at me.

"No, I meant that he hasn't had anyone here at all. I don't think he's even touched any of the bunnies here. Do you like him?"

"I-I've never had a boyfriend. I had a boy friend and one day he asked me out. My father heard him and got really angry. After that, Bryce never spoke to me again. And what exactly is a 'bunny'?"

I thought I would see pity in Luciana's eyes. Instead I see anger.

"First of all, your parents are assholes. I'm so sorry they treated you and Lucy the way they did. I can't even imagine what that was like for you. And well, a 'bunny' is a woman that hangs around our club and is willing to sleep with club members."

"Wow. And the bunnies don't mind doing that? Why would they do that willingly? As for my parents? We got away. That's what's helping me now, knowing they can't hurt me or Lucy now. But I do worry that they'll find us."

"You don't need to worry about that. If they come to Lake Renegade and try to cause problems? They're not going to like what they find. We take care of each other here. Oh and the women? They're hoping one of the patched members will want them as their 'old lady.' The one they choose to be with. And no. I'm not an 'old lady.'" She chuckles.

I laugh. "I guess I'll need to learn all these terms."

She nods. "You will, club life isn't for everyone. And it's okay if you don't want to be with the club, we are family in the club and outside of it."

I smile. If Romano is part of the club, that's what I want. I don't want to follow him around like a little lost puppy. I want him, and I want him to want me.

"And yes, I think Romano likes you too." She nudges me.

"Why do you think I like him?" I ask, trying to put on my most innocent look.

Luciana laughs. "Because you haven't taken your eyes off him. And I saw you when Chelsea touched him."

So the bunny has a name. Chelsea. Ugh. She can't have him.

"You think he would really be interested in me? What if I can't give him what he wants?"

"What do you mean? I've learned a few things about Romano. One? He's loyal as any of us, he will protect you—and us—with everything he has. Two? If you're thinking because you've never been in a relationship that he would think less of you? No way. Not Romano. I think if you're the one for him, he'll treat you like a queen."

"Thank you, Luciana." I smile more. Maybe I really could be with Romano.

I look around for Lucy and see her playing with Saoirse and Maddie. They're feeding the otters, and it's the most adorable thing I've seen in a while. I don't think I've ever seen Lucy smile and laugh so much. It makes my heart so happy to see her having fun.

"Are you doing okay?"

I whip my head around and face Romano. "I

am. I was just watching Lucy. I've never seen her so happy before."

"I hope that you'll see her like this from now on," he says. His hand brushes mine and I look down at it. "I promise I won't hurt you."

Somehow I know this deep in my soul. I may not have any experience, but I know how I feel about him. And I know he would never intentionally hurt me. I look up into his eyes and nod.

"I know you won't. I don't know how I know, but I feel it in here." I put my hand over my heart.

Romano wraps his arms around me and my world feels whole and safe. This is where I'm meant to be, I just know it.

Romano

Holding Simone in my arms like this is something I thought I'd never do. Holding another woman. But it feels right. She could never take the place of Amara. But being with Simone feels like the next chapter of my life is beginning. I was prepared to be alone for the rest of my life. Now I feel like I've been given a second chance at love.

And if I'm reading her right, she feels the same way about me.

"Have you ever had a relationship?" I ask her softly.

Simone shakes her head no.

"My parents wouldn't allow us to date or even talk to boys."

"How old are you?"

Caitríona told me how old she is, but I want her to open up to me.

"I'm twenty-one, I'll be twenty-two soon. How old are you?" she asks, looking up at me with her big cerulean blue eyes.

"I'm twenty-six, soon to be twenty-seven. When is your birthday?"

"October seventh."

Holy fuck.

"That's my birthday too." I smile.

"Really?" Her eyes get even bigger.

I chuckle.

"We can celebrate together, we'll have a party here. It'll be a lot of fun, we like celebrating birthdays and special occasions."

"I've never had a birthday party. We usually just got a few presents and my mother would make our favorite dinner and dessert."

"Well this year you're going to have the biggest party ever."

Simone's smile lights up her face. "I can't wait!"

"When is Lucy's birthday? She turns eighteen, right? That's a big milestone."

Simone nods. "Her birthday is in February. Do you think it would be okay to throw her a surprise party?"

"That would be a lot of fun, I bet all the women would love to help you plan that."

"I can't wait to see her face. She'd never expect something like that. Hey, Romano? Can I ask you something?"

"You can ask me anything."

"How come you don't have a girlfriend? Or a wife? I see the women here watching you, and I can tell they want you. But you're here with me..."

I take a deep breath. I guess it's as good a time as any to tell her about my family...and my loss.

"It's a long story, why don't we sit down and I'll tell you about me."

I take Simone's hand and lead her to one of the empty tables. I sit next to her and face her, I want her to know that what I went through will always be with me. But that I hope that she wants to be a part of my future.

"I had a wife and three children. Bruno was seven, Romeo was five and Oriana was three. I lost all of them a year and a half ago in Italy. I moved here six months after it happened because everywhere I went, all I saw was my family. I told myself that I would never go through that again. I was okay being alone."

Simone is looking at me with tears streaming down her face. I wipe some away and kiss her hand.

"I'm so sorry, Romano. I can't even imagine what that's like to lose your whole family."

"I learned afterwards that Amara was three months pregnant."

Simone gasps and grips my hand tighter.

"When it happened I said 'no more.' I would live my life with my club and that was enough for me. But then I saw you crossing the street yesterday. And you flipped my world around. Suddenly I saw a different future. One that incudes you, if you want to be in it."

Simone scoots closer to me on the bench.

"I would never force you to be with me. But I do hope you feel for me what I feel for you. I know it's only been a day, and I can hear myself and I know I sound crazy."

She wraps her arms around me and squeezes

me tight.

"I don't know how to be in a relationship, but if you don't mind being patient with me...I want to learn with you."

She can't see the smile that's on my face, but I look over and see Luciana smiling at us.

"Yes, we will learn together," I say as I squeeze her tight and she giggles.

Caitríona comes over and sits across from us.

"Simone, we were all wondering if you'd like to come and live on the property with us. I know you're worried about your parents coming for you. If you and Lucy live here, we can protect you better."

Simones eyes fill with tears as she listens to Caitríona.

"I don't know what to say. When we left, we didn't know where we were going or how we were going to live. And by chance we stopped here in Lake Renegade. At first we were only going to stay for a few days, but I told myself that if I could find a job, then we would stay longer."

"And then you came into our bakery and the rest is history." Caitríona smiles. "So is that a 'yes'? We have a cottage that would be perfect for you and Lucy. It has two bedrooms, two bathrooms, a living room and kitchen."

"How much will it be monthly?" Simone asks Caitríona.

"You won't pay any rent. The money you make at the bakery? You save it and use it for whatever you or Lucy need."

"What about electricity and water?"

"Baby, that's all taken care of. You and Lucy will move in and not have any worries. We'll even get a tutor to help Lucy get her diploma. Then she can decide if she wants to go to college. In fact, if you want, you can go to college for baking."

I watch Simone as she listens to Caitríona. I don't think she's ever had any choices in her life. That thought makes me so fucking angry. Who does this to their children? Keep them locked up with no life but to serve their parents. One day I will be paying her parents a visit.

"Can I talk to Lucy before I give you an answer? I don't want to make any decisions for her. That's what our parents did and I promised myself that if we ever got out, I would be different."

"Of course. Take your time. The offer has no time limit, we just want you to know that you're safe. Even if you both want to stay at the Hideaway for a bit, we'll still be there to protect you." Caitríona smiles.

Chapter Seven

Simone

I plan on talking to Lucy tonight after we get back to our room. I'm still in shock that Caitríona would offer something like this to us. They don't even know us, yet they're willing to help us. I dreamed of finding a place like this, but it was just a dream. And Romano. Every time he touches me or holds me, my body molds to him. He's something I never even let myself dream of. He's so handsome, sea-green eyes, dark wavy hair, tall, muscles everywhere. And the best part? He makes me feel wanted. It's a new feeling and one that I hope never goes away.

I've read about sex in romance books that I borrowed on my tablet. The one thing I was allowed to have was that, and I was allowed to borrow books. My parents saw the books I borrowed, but for some reason they never said anything about them. Books have always been my escape. I read all kinds of books, but the romance ones were my favorite. Big tattooed men who love their women with everything in them. I would have dreams of finding my one. They said in my books that you just know when you meet them. Well Romano makes me feel that way. Like he was meant to be mine. I just wish I knew how to help him get through his sadness about his family. I know he said he wants to be with me, but I can still see the sadness in his eyes.

"I'll drive you and Lucy back to the Hideaway when you're ready," Romano says as he takes my hand and kisses it.

"Thank you, that would be really nice."

I wonder what it would be like to kiss him? It would be my first kiss ever. And the more I think about it, the more I want it.

"What are you thinking about?" Romano quietly asks me.

I tilt my head to look up at him, wondering if I should tell him the truth or not.

"I was wondering what it would feel like for you to kiss me," I whisper.

"Have you ever been kissed?"

I shake my head no. I watch him slowly lower his head towards mine and I close my eyes. When our lips touch, it's like my whole body comes alive. He slides his tongue along my lower lip, I open my mouth slightly and he deepens the kiss. My brain is firing faster and when he pulls back, all I can say is...

"Wow."

I wrap my arms around him and breathe him in.

"Thank you. That was better than what I dreamed of when I read my books."

Romano smiles at me. "What kind of books?"

"My romance books. They always say how when you kiss the right person, no one else will ever compare to it."

"Well you won't be kissing anyone else. So I hope that kissing me made you feel the way it made me feel—"

"Alive." We both say together.

Romano

Simone makes me feel alive. She's awakened the parts of me that I was sure were gone for good. When I kissed her, I could feel my heart beating like it was going to pop out of my chest. And I wasn't kidding when I told her that she wouldn't be kissing any other man. I don't care how long it takes, but I will be the first and last man for her.

It's like I can hear Amara saying 'it's okay to love someone again.' She'll always be a part of me and who I am. But Amara is part of my past, and Simone is my future.

"Are you ready to head back to your hotel room?" I ask Simone.

"I am. I need to talk to Lucy about living here."

"Do you have a cell phone?"

"No. I was hoping to get one after I get paid."

"I'll be right back, then we can leave."

"Okay. I'll let Lucy know we're ready to go."

I give her a quick kiss and head towards Giacomo. When I get to him, he's grinning at me.

"What?" I frown.

"You've been here for a while now and I don't think I've ever seen you smile this much."

I make a noise at him. "I smile."

"Not like you do when you look at Simone." He chuckles.

I sigh at him. "Do we still have extra cell

phones? Simone and Lucy don't have phones. And I was hoping I could give them one."

"We do. Franco has them, he's been keeping track of them. Plus we now have trackers in them for extra security."

I nod. "Thanks, I'll go ask him."

"Hey, Romano?"

"Yeah?" I say, turning back to Giacomo.

"I'm glad you're happy. You know that Amara wouldn't want you to be alone forever, right?" he says, taking the two steps between us and giving me a hug. "I hope it's okay—Caitríona told me about your family. She was afraid you might be upset because she said she wouldn't tell anyone."

"Thanks, it's okay. I know you two have no secrets. Amara and I were like that. And I'm beginning to get that feeling too. At first I thought I had my one-and-only chance. I never thought I'd get a second one."

"Good people deserve all the chances in the world." He smiles, hugging me one more time, then heads towards Caitríona.

I don't know if I'm a good person, but I do hope that I deserve someone like Simone. She's so damn beautiful, but so innocent. I don't want to hurt her. Time to find Franco for the phone..

"Hey Franco, I need two cell phones. They're for Simone and Lucy."

"Sure. Give me a minute to get them set up. Did you want me to put any numbers in them?"

"Yeah, can we put the women's numbers and mine in both? That way if they need anything, they can call any of us."

"Sure thing." He starts clicking away at his computer. "So...you look happy out there with the new girl, Simone."

"For fucks sake, not you too." I sigh.

Franco laughs as he keeps clicking his keyboard. "We're just happy for you."

"Thank you. It means a lot to have everyone's support with this."

"You're family. We got each other's backs."

"I made the right decision when I asked to transfer here. You've all made everything better for me."

Franco smiles and finishes up what he's doing.

"Okay, I programmed the phones and activated them on the family plan. So they don't have to worry about anything. And if they have any issues, tell them to come to me."

I nod. "Thanks again, Franco."

"Not a problem. Drive safe."

I park the car in the Hideaway lot and get out to open the doors for Simone and Lucy.

"Can you come up with us and wait while I talk to Lucy?" Simone asks.

"Of course. If she says yes, do you want to go back with me tonight?"

"I do. And I think she'll say yes." She smiles up at me.

I lean down and kiss her, and we hear Lucy giggle.

"You two are cute." She smiles at us.

"Thank you." I chuckle. "Let's get upstairs and out of the cold."

We all walk upstairs to their room.

"I'll wait here while you talk to Lucy," I say to Simone.

She takes Lucy to the bedroom and I turn the TV on to give them some privacy.

Simone

"Is something wrong?" Lucy asks me as we go into her room.

"No, nothing's wrong. But I do have something I want to talk to you about. And it's a big thing. Caitríona has offered us a home on their property. She says it's a two bedroom, two bath cottage. And that they will help you get your diploma."

Lucy's eyes get wider with each thing I tell her.

"Are you serious? Do you want to move there?"

"I do. But I want to know what you want. Do you want to move there? Did you have a good feeling when we were there tonight?"

Lucy stops and thinks for a minute.

"I did have a good feeling there. It felt like they all cared about us, but they don't even know us. I never thought there were really people like that."

"And they like to hug. A lot." I chuckle.

"They do!" She giggles. "And I know you like Romano. From what I can see, he really likes you too. I can't believe you got your first kiss. I hope one day I find my person."

"You will. It may take some time, but I know you'll find someone that will treat you the way Romano treats me."

"How do you know after only a day?"

"I don't know how to explain it. It feels like he's a part of me, that no matter what, he's who I need.

Let's pack up and get checked out. We can talk more when we get to our new home."

"Home."

Lucy jumps up and squeezes me tight.

"Thank you for not leaving me behind," she whispers.

"I'd never leave you, Lucy. We're a team, no matter what."

I head back to the room to pack my stuff. Lucy's in the bathroom grabbing everything in there. I feel the air shift as Romano walks in, I don't need to turn around to know he's there.

"I see you're packing, does this mean Lucy said yes?"

"She did. Are you sure it's okay for us to be there? I don't want to impose."

Romano's big hands turn me around to face him. I love looking at him, I could stare at him all day.

"Caitríona doesn't offer things like this to everyone. She will help anyone, but to invite them into our lives? That's a completely different situation. So yes, I'm sure that it's okay for you to be there."

"Is it possible to live close to you?" I say softly as I look at my feet.

He tilts my chin to look up at him.

"I wouldn't want you to live anywhere but close to me," he says as he leans down and takes my lips again. This time I part my lips to give him access and I can't help the moan that escapes. I run my hands down his back, I can feel his muscles through his shirt. I wonder what he looks like without his shirt on...

"Baby," he pants as he takes his lips away from mine. "I want you so damn bad. But the first time I make love to you? It won't be in a motel room."

My whole body is responding to him in ways I've never felt. I learned about sex from my books and from school. But I've never thought I'd meet someone like Romano. Someone that makes me want to rip his clothes off and do all those things I read in my books. Great. Now all I can think about is what he would look like naked. And I can feel the heat rising in my face.

"I want you, Romano. But I don't know if I would be what you want..." I trail off.

"Simone, look at me."

I raise my eyes back up to his.

"You are perfect the way you are. We will take things at your pace, and we'll learn together."

"But you know what you want. You've been with other women."

"I've been with one woman. I've never been with anyone but Amara."

I search his eyes to see if he's lying to me. The look in his eyes is telling me that he's not lying to me.

"I met Amara when we were fourteen. She was my first and only till now."

"What about the club bunnies? Luciana said that they're there for the men to enjoy."

"They're not for me to enjoy. I've never touched them."

"What about the one that was near you tonight? Luciana said her name was Chelsea."

I try to keep the jealousy out of my voice, but it's hard. I saw what Chelsea looked like, she was really pretty and I can see why men would want her.

"Chelsea has been trying to get me to sleep with her since I got here. But I've never touched her."

I frown at him. I want to believe him, but I saw some of the other men with the bunnies too. Then again, Romano has never given me a reason not to trust him. So I need to believe him.

"Promise?"

"I promise you, Simone. I have never touched anyone after Amara. And you will be the only one I'll be with from now on."

I wrap my arms around him, I can barely touch my fingers together as I hold him. I love how protected I feel in his arms. I've never felt safe before. Not like this.

Chapter Eight

Romano

While Simone and Lucy pack up their stuff, I call Caitríona and let her know that I'm bringing them back with me. She's really happy that they decided to come and live on the property. They're getting the cottage that's closest to mine ready. I want to ask Simone if she'd like to live with me. But before I do that, maybe she needs to live on her own for a bit. The waiting is going to be really hard. But I think it's the best way, she needs to know that she's strong and can do this. Her parents took away her voice, I want to give it back to her.

"Okay, I'm ready," Lucy says as she comes out of the bathroom.

"If you forget anything, they'll get it to you. Perks of living in a small town." I chuckle.

Lucy comes over to me and whispers, "Please be good to Simone. She could've left me when Thomas and Robin left. But she stayed with me, and even when my father was hitting her? She stayed for me."

Anger is bubbling up in me when Lucy says their father beat Simone. I will find that man and show him what it feels like to be beaten. Fucking coward beating his daughter. He'll be lucky to be able to walk when I'm done with him.

"I'm ready too," Simone says, coming out of the room.

"The women are getting your house together, it should be ready by the time we get there. They're really excited that you're coming to live with all of us."

"I don't know how to thank all of you for everything."

"I keep meaning to ask you, why did you pick Lake Renegade?"

"I thought it sounded nice. Lucy got excited about there being a lake. So we decided to stop here first. And if I couldn't find a job, we would try somewhere else. When we got here, I saw Precious Risings Bakery. It felt right. And when I went in and talked to Rosaura, she hired me on the spot. All she asked is if I've worked in a bakery before. I never thought we'd be this lucky."

I hug my Simone tight. "I'm really happy that you chose Lake Renegade."

"Hey! I helped too!" Lucy raises her eyebrow at us.

I grab her and add her to our hug. I love the giggles coming from both of them. With every smile and every laugh, they're helping my heart heal.

"Okay, let's get you checked out and to your new home."

"Yes! Will we be living near you?" Lucy asks as we get into the elevator.

"Yep. And near Francesco and Mitchell."

"Oh! That's fun! I love Saoirse, she's adorable," Lucy cheers. "And the otters! I can't wait to get to know them more."

I laugh. "Those otters are the best. The original otter family is back in Ireland. That's where Francesco got the idea for this family. We're actually a registered otter sanctuary, so we can take in ones that need a home."

"That's so awesome. Maybe I could go to school to work with animals." Lucy smiles.

When we get down to the counter to check out, Chelsea comes out. I see Simone stiffen up next to me, I take her hand in mine and kiss it.

"Hey Chelsea, Simone needs to check out of her room. It's room six-oh-one."

I watch Chelsea look at Simone and Lucy and frown.

"Sure, Fantasma. They still have a balance to pay."

I hand her my credit card. Which makes her glare at Simone.

"Do we have a problem?" I ask.

"Uh, no. sorry."

"I have money to pay," Simone whispers to me.

"I know, but you're mine and I want to help you."

Chelsea snorts when I call Simone mine. And that pisses me the fuck off. I can see the doubt in Simone's face when she does that and it pisses me off even more.

"Are you done?" I snap at Chelsea.

She hands me a receipt and my card.

"Okay, let's go." I take both of their bags and we head out to the car.

"See you soon, Fantasma," Chelsea calls out.

I'm going to have a talk with Giacomo about her as soon as I get them settled.

Simone

That girl Chelsea keeps making faces at me and staring at Romano. I don't know why she called him 'Fantasma.' But she makes me feel so insecure and I don't like it.

"Why did Chelsea call you 'Fantasma'?" I ask him once we're in the car.

"It's my road name. Everyone in the MC has a road name. They're given to us by our president, I got mine when I was in Italy."

"What does it mean?"

"It means 'ghost.' I'm good at being quiet and getting in and out of places."

They both laugh.

"So does that mean you were a bad person before?" Lucy asks.

"Lucy!" Simone exclaims.

"What?" She has a scared look on her face.

He chuckles. "It's okay. And no, I wasn't a bad person. I was given that name because my president said that I could sneak up on any of them."

Lucy giggles in the back seat. "I bet you can't sneak up on me."

"We'll see. I'm pretty good at sneaking around."

I love seeing Lucy so relaxed and having a good time. We had fun growing up when it was the four of us. But whenever our parents were with us, we had to be on our best behavior. We were all scared of our father, even if he didn't hit us back then. I feel safe when I'm with Romano, but I'm still worried that our parents will find us and make us go back with them. If they came for Lucy, I'd have to go too. I'll never leave her alone.

Romano

The Cimaruta MC has one prospect right now, Anthony Grimes. A few months ago, he was shot in a territory battle that was going on. We were lucky that he came out of his coma and is doing well. He's on gate duty tonight, it's basically light duty for him.

"Everything good?" I ask him as we stop at the gate.

"Yep. All good." He smiles.

"This is Simone and Lucy, they'll be staying on the property from now on. If anyone comes asking about them, you don't know them. Let one of us know right away."

"Got it. Forza gave me the rundown too. I got your back, brother."

"Thank you," I say as we drive in. I can see the gates closing behind us. It takes a minute to drive them to their cottage.

"This is yours. Mine is right over there, Franco is to the left and Mitchell to the right," I tell them as we get out.

"Wow! Your houses are really big!" Lucy exclaims.

"One day you'll have something bigger than the cottage," I say to her.

I park in front of their cottage and get out. I grab their bags and follow them to the front door. Before we get there, it bursts open and all the women come tumbling out to greet Simone and Lucy. The smiles on the girls' faces are worth everything. I wait outside as they're shown around the cottage. There are several cottages on the

Bastianini property. We use them when other chapter clubs come to visit.

After everyone goes back to their houses, I head inside to give them their bags.

"This place is perfect." Lucy smiles as she runs around the cottage.

Simone comes over to me and wraps her arms around me.

"Thank you for all this," she says softly.

"I didn't do anything. I'm just here to help you."

"You make me feel safe. I've never truly felt safe before."

Hearing her say that makes my heart hurt for her. I know that she'll never feel unsafe again.

"You'll always be safe with me. I promise," I say as I kiss her head. I feel her body relax in my arms. Holding her makes my body come alive and I'm pretty sure she can feel my cock pressing into her side. She looks up at me with her big blue eyes.

"It's not a secret that I want you," I whisper to her. "I wasn't lying when I said I would wait for you. But you need to know how much I want you."

Simone runs her hands on my chest and it makes me growl. Her eyes get bigger and she smiles at me.

"I want you too, Romano. I'm just afraid you

won't like me because I've never been with anyone."

"That doesn't matter. I told you, I will be your first and last. So your experience doesn't matter to me."

She nods and I squeeze her tighter.

"You and Lucy should get some rest. If you need me, you call me or come to my place."

"Okay, thank you."

I lean down and kiss her, I try to show her how much I want her in that kiss.

"Omg. Kissing again?" Lucy giggles.

"I'll see you two in the morning." I laugh.

Romano

I walk to my house, thinking of Simone the whole way. I'm doing my best not to push her to do something she's not ready for. But holy fuck, it's hard. As soon as I get home I head to my shower. Hopefully a cold one will help me for now. I stand under the cold water until I start to shiver slightly. I can't stop thinking of Simone and it's starting to make me crazy.

I get out and hear a knock at my door. I grab my towel and wrap it around my waist. I'm dripping, but fuck it. I don't know who would be knocking at my door at this hour.

When I open the door, it's definitely not who I was expecting.

"Is everything okay?" I ask Simone as I open the door wider so she can come in.

Her eyes never leave my chest as she walks in. I'm a little worried because she's not saying anything. Just staring at me.

"You have a lot of tattoos," she finally says.

My arms, chest and back are covered with tattoos. I have a back piece that's a tribute to Amara and my children. And my chest is covered with the Cimaruta cross and a few pieces I got back in Italy. Simone reaches out and traces the Cimaruta cross on my chest. Her touch makes me instantly hard again. Fuck me.

She looks down at my towel and then back up at me. She runs her hand down my chest and stops right above my towel.

"Are you sure about this?" I whisper. "Because once I start, I don't think I can stop myself. Also after we make love, you're mine. And only mine."

Simone moves closer to me and takes her coat off. Holy fuck. All she's wearing is a tank top and shorts. I reach out and pull her to me.

"Are you sure?" I ask again. I need to hear her say what she wants.

"I want you, Romano. All I know is what I've

read in my books. And how you make me feel. You make me want to do things I've never really thought about before. So yes. I'm sure. I want you to be my first and last."

That's all I need to hear, I pick her up and take her to my bed. I need to remember to try and take it slow with her. But all I can think about right now is her pregnant with our baby. Fast? Maybe.

I place her on the bed and help her out of her tank top and shorts.

"You're fucking beautiful."

"I want to see you. Please."

Who am I to deny her anything? I slowly loosen my towel and let it drop to the floor. She gasps softly. I get on the bed next to her. I start nibbling on her neck and that makes her moan. It might be my new favorite sound.

Simone

When Romano was holding me earlier, I could feel his cock against my tummy. And it made me wet down there. I've read about it, but to feel it...I wanted him right there. But I had to wait. After he left, I couldn't stop thinking about it so I took a fast shower and decided I was going to go over to his house. I wasn't going to wait any longer.

Seeing him naked is a whole other thing. I feel like I'm dripping as he kisses and bites at my neck. I reach down and wrap my hand around his cock.

"Fuck," he moans.

"Show me what you like."

"Baby, if you keep touching me like that, this will be over before I can show you what I like."

I can't help the giggle that escapes me. Knowing I have that effect on him is turning me on even more. I want to feel him inside me, but I don't know if he'll fit.

"I want to feel you inside me," I say as I look into his beautiful eyes that look like they're still changing colors.

"Are you sure?" he asks again.

This is the third time he's asked me if I'm sure. I think he's afraid that I'll regret being with him, but I won't. Not now, not ever.

"I choose you, Romano. And I hope you choose me too."

Romano

"Simone, I choose you today and forever," I say as I lick my way down her body. I want to taste her before I make her mine. I get down to her clit and slowly suck it into my mouth.

"Oh my god," she gasps.

I slowly slide a finger in her as I keep sucking on her clit. I can feel her orgasm coming. When she explodes, it's the most beautiful thing I've ever seen. As she's coming down from it, I slowly position the head of my cock at her opening.

"I need you to look at me, baby," I say as she opens her eyes and looks at me. "It might hurt a little, you tell me and I'll do my best to slow down."

She nods as I slowly push into her. I can feel myself leaking pre-cum as I move more.

"Are you okay?" I ask as I continue to push into her.

"Are you all the way in?" she whispers.

"No, do you want me to stop?"

"No please don't stop."

I finally seat myself as far into her as I can. And it's fucking heaven, she's so damn tight. I'm pretty sure I'm only going to get a few strokes in before I'm done. I start to move more, but she's squeezing my cock so fucking much. I move slowly so that she can get used to me. But fuck me, I can feel the cum trying to force its way out of me. I need to last a little longer. Her moans are driving me insane.

"I need to feel you come," I moan, sliding my hand between us and circling her clit. I feel her clenching tighter. Fuck me.

She explodes on my cock as I push as far into her as I can. Her pussy is milking every last drop out of cum out of my cock.

The first thought I have when my mind clears is that she could get pregnant. And that thought makes me puff up my chest with pride. I know it's fast, but I also know she's it for me.

"Um. Romano?" she asks in a tiny voice.

"Yes, love?"

"I'm not on birth control, and we didn't use a condom." She sniffles.

"Please don't cry. I want this. You. Us. Babies."

She looks up at me. "You do?"

"I told you that once we make love, I'm yours and you're mine. I don't want anyone but you."

I haven't pulled out of her yet. I know that the longer I can keep my cum in her, the better chance we have of her getting pregnant.

"I dreamed of meeting you. I always thought it was just a dream. But now you're here. You're real."

I smile and kiss her. "After I lost Amara, I told

myself I was done. But now that I've met you? I know that there's another part to my life. And that life will be with you."

She snuggles against me and I hold her tight. I say a silent thank you to Amara for sending Simone to me. Because I know this is because of her.

Chapter Ten

Simone

I yawn and stretch, my body is a little sore. But then I remember making love to Romano. How gentle he was with me. He says that I'm his now, and I hope he means it. I wasn't lying when I said that I dreamed of him. When I would read my romance books, I wished for someone like him. I told myself that it was just a dream and that no matter what I wanted it would stay a dream.

Now here he is and he's even more than my dream. He's tall and broad, covered in gorgeous tattoos. I thought that when I had sex for the first time, it would hurt a lot. But Romano was so gentle with me that it only hurt at the beginning. Then it felt so good, better than anything I've ever felt. I don't know if all men are as big as he is and from what he says, I'll never know. And that's okay with me. He also says he wants to have babies with me. That scares me, yet it excites me.

"Morning, mia farfalla," he says as he stretches.

"What does 'mia farfalla' mean?" I ask as I lay my head on his chest.

"'My butterfly.' You started as a caterpillar locked in your cocoon. And now you're a beautiful butterfly. My butterfly."

I giggle. "I love that. And I love you, Romano. I know it's fast and you don't have to say it back. But I really do love you. You're making my dreams come true one at a time."

He turns to look at me. "I love you, mia farfalla. I am so grateful that you've come into my life."

I turn and look at the clock, it's three in the morning.

"Do you need to get back for Lucy?" he asks me.

I nod. "I should. I told her I was coming here and she has her phone."

"Move in with me. I know you just moved into your cottage. But I want you and Lucy her with me."

I look into his eyes. "Are you sure? You don't have to do that, knowing you love me is more than I could ask for right now"

"I do want it. I don't want you far from me and the cottage is too far."

I laugh. "It's a one-minute walk."

"And that's a minute I don't get to spend with you," he says as he pouts at me, then starts nibbling on my neck. Which makes me laugh even more.

"You're such a goofball."

He stops nibbling. 'Goofball huh?" He laughs and tickles me. I've always hated when my siblings and I would get into tickle fights. But Romano doing it? I'll take it. "My girl is ticklish. I love it."

"Are you?" I laugh even more.

"Nope," he says. So I try and tickle him and I get nothing. Well crap.

"That's not fair." I pout back at him.

He chuckles and kisses me, sucking on my pouty lip. It makes me want him again, but I'm a bit sore down there and I don't know if I can. It's like he can sense my hesitation.

"It's okay, baby. You need to rest a little before we make love again. Maybe tonight." He gives me a mischievous smile.

He's too much, but I can't stop smiling at him. He makes me feel so happy. And I don't remember a time when I was this happy. Or this free. For the first time, I feel like I can do anything. I have a job, a new home and Romano. When I dreamed of leaving, all I wished for was a job and a roof over my head. And for Lucy. Maybe one day we will find Thomas and Robin, that would make everything complete. I think about them daily and hope that they're doing alright.

___

Romano

___

I can see the wheels turning in my girl's head.

"What's going on in that beautiful head of yours?"

"I was thinking that I wish I could find Thomas and Robin. But I don't know if they've changed their names, or what direction they went when they left. It makes me sad to think that I might not ever see them again."

"I didn't want to say anything until I knew something solid. But I asked Franco to look into finding them for you. It may take a while. But we're hoping they kept their names, and if not? We'll do our best to find them for you and Lucy."

"Thank you so much. I don't know what I did to deserve you, but I'm so glad I found you."

"Did your parents let any of you out of the house alone?"

Simone shakes her head no. "We were only allowed to go to church with them. That was four times a week. And sometimes to the store. But never alone."

"I need you to tell me what made you leave now. What happened to you or to Lucy?"

She takes a deep breath. "Nothing bad happened until Thomas and Robin left. My father never really yelled at us or raised a hand to us. And my mother just made us do things with her. Clean, cook, sew, those kinds of things. But then one day Thomas told us he had to go. That he couldn't stay any longer. Lucy was only sixteen, Robin had just turned eighteen so she decided she wanted to go with him. As much as I wanted to go too, I couldn't leave Lucy. Thomas was allowed to work with our father on what he called 'side jobs.' They would go to peoples homes and do repair work or even just mow their lawns or pool stuff. So he was allowed to keep some of his money. Before he left, he gave me money and said to hide it really well. So I did. That's how we were able to take the bus here and pay for the hotel."

"You said nothing bad happened until Thomas left. What happened to you, mia farfalla? I need you to tell me."

This time she tears up and my anger is rising. What the fuck did her father do to her? Whatever he did to her, I'm going to do to him twice as bad.

"First he started yelling at me, mostly little things. Pillows or a fork was out of place. Then one time I was late with dinner because I forgot to turn the oven on. That was the first time he hit me. But he never touched Lucy, so I was glad for that. I gladly took whatever he was going to do as long as he left her alone."

I sit up and look at Simone. "You know that no matter what you've done, you didn't deserve to be hit by him. Your father is an asshole and a coward for hitting you. Fathers are supposed to protect their children, not hurt them."

"I'm still afraid they're going to find us and force us to go back with them."

"That's never going to happen. You and Lucy are safe."

I want to tell her about our families, but until she's my wife, I can't. Which will happen soon, but until then, I can't. Wife. That's a word I didn't think would come out of my mouth ever again. And the thought of having more babies used to scare me. With Simone? It doesn't.

"I know you need to get back to Lucy. I'll walk you back over. And from now on? No walking at night alone. Call or text me, I'll come get you. Okay?"

"Okay, but why? I thought we were safe here?"

"You are. But there's always something that *could* happen. And I don't want to take that chance with you."

"Thank you. I've never felt like I was wanted, you make me feel wanted."

That one little statement makes me want to kill her parents even more. One day I will be face to face with them and I'll show them what I think of their 'parenting.'

We get up and I can't keep my eyes off of her as she gets dressed. She's so much more than I deserve to have. But for some reason, I found her and she chose me. I'm a lucky bastard.

Chapter Eleven

Simone

It's been about a month since Lucy and I came to Lake Renegade. Last weekend we moved into Romano's home. I wanted to give Lucy the ability to choose things, our parents always made the choices for us. I can see how much Lucy has started to relax since we've been here. She laughs a lot and runs around with the little kids. she's seventeen but we were never allowed to be kids. So I can't stop smiling when I watch her. She's just so carefree.

Today we're at one of the Cimaruta MC's barbecues. There are members from some of the other chapters here, I've been trying to remember all their names. It's not easy. But they're all really nice.

"Hi, my love," Romano says as he comes up behind me. I lean back and feel him behind me. His arms come around and cage me in. This is my favorite place, wrapped in his strong arms. I haven't told him yet, but I think I'm pregnant. I'm two weeks late for my period. And I've never been late before. Romano always tells me that he wants me pregnant, and I can't say that scares me. What scares me is what if he changes his mind? I know he's still hurting from losing his family. I've noticed that each day that we spend together, he relaxes a little more. I don't want him to ever forget his family, he tells me stories of them. How he and Amara met, how it was for him to be a papà for the first time.

I turn around in his arms to face him.

"So I have something I need to tell you. Now I'm not positive, but I'm like ninety percent su—."

"Are you pregnant?" He's smiling.

I laugh. "I think I might be. I've never been late, but I'm two weeks late now."

He picks me up gently and hugs me. "You don't know how happy you've made me."

When he puts me down, he places his hand on

my belly. He looks so happy, I can't help but smile more.

"Marry me, mia farfalla. I want to give you and our bambino a full life. One where you'll never have to worry about anything."

Everyone's starting to gather around us.

"Yes. I will marry you."

***

Romano

***

Simone lets out a squeal as I pick her up again. Still being careful of her belly. I wonder if she got pregnant that first night we were together. Either way, I've gotten what I want. A beautiful wife and a baby to cherish. I'm lucky that Simone is okay with how I am. I was possessive with Amara. But Simone? I don't want her out of my sight. Which gets hard because of my bodyguard duties and the fact that she's working at the bakery. Now that she's officially my fiancée, I need to ask one of my club brothers to be her bodyguard. I plan on bringing it up at our next council meeting, which is today. I'll also need to tell my club about what Simone and Lucy have been through. So in case their parents find them here, everyone's prepared.

After everyone goes back to the barbecue, I slip the ring I got her on her finger.

"Oh my goodness. This is the most beautiful ring I've ever seen," she says softly.

I had it custom made for her. It has a butterfly that's made up from all different jewels. I wanted her to have an original engagement ring. And we will pick out our wedding rings together. I want her to be my wife before we have our baby.

"I'll be back," I say to her as Forza calls for church.

The clubhouse is filled because this barbecue is a mandatory one. That means every chapter associated with the Cimaruta MC is here. Including the European chapters. First we have our council meeting to catch up with all the chapter clubs. Nothing new is going on right now and that's such a relief. In the last year, our club has gone through a lot. There's been kidnappings, old grudges coming back up and we almost lost a few members.

"I'm glad to hear that no one is having any major issues right now. After the year we've had? This quiet time is welcomed," Giacomo 'Forza' Bastianini says. He is the president of our club, and we are the mother club. The original Cimaruta MC.

The room gets quiet as each chapter president updates us on what's going on. This process takes about an hour to get through everyone. After we're done, the other chapters head back out to the barbecue and we stay to have our meeting.

"You all know that we have two new women living on the property, Simone and Lucy Young. And you also know that Simone is Fantasma's woman. We all saw earlier that he's asked her to be his wife. So I wanted to take this time to congratulate him."

All my brothers get up and give me a hug.

"Grazie. I have one request. Now that Simone will be my wife, I would like to ask for someone to be her bodyguard. You should all know her story, and she's given me permission to tell you."

I tell everyone about what Simone and Lucy have gone through. The room is dead silent as they all listen. My brothers think like me. No man should lay a hand on a woman. especially not a father.

"I will be Simone's bodyguard," Brennan 'Raziel' Doyle says. He is the club chaplain.

"Thank you." I nod to him. "I have one more thing to say, Simone is pregnant."

All the guys start cheering.

"Damn, that was fast," Hollis 'Cavallo' Taylor, another enforcer teases.

"Are we going to go after her asshole parents?" Bestia asks.

"In time, I think we will find them and make sure they stay away. Right now, I don't know if Simone or Lucy could handle it," I say to him.

"I agree, we need to make sure the girls are okay before we find their parents," Forza says.

We wrap things up and head back out to the barbecue. I head straight for my baby, she's standing with Rosaura.

"Congratulations, Romano." Rosaura smiles as she hugs me.

"Thank you."

"I told Rosaura about the baby. I couldn't wait." Simone giggles. I love how excited she is, I lay my hand on her belly. I can't wait till she's showing.

"I told the club too." I chuckle. "Also, Raziel will be with you when I can't."

Simone looks at me. "I get a bodyguard now? Why?"

"Because you're going to be my wife and you're pregnant with our child. That's how it works in this family."

"Okay," she says as she hugs me.

"Thank you for not arguing with me about it."

"I know that anything you do is good for me, the baby and Lucy. I've been controlled before. You're the opposite of that."

I hold her tight. When she's ready, I will be paying her parents a visit. They have to be taught a lesson, and they will learn.

Chapter Twelve

Simone

Time feels like it's flying by really fast. It's been four months since we found our new home. And three months since Romano asked me to marry him. We're getting married next month. He wants me to carry his name before our baby is born. And today we get to see our baby in an ultrasound. We've been trying to decide if we want to know if we're having a boy or girl. I kind of do, but I kind of don't. Romano says maybe we should wait, we still have time to decide.

Every morning, Romano, Lucy and I have breakfast together. Then Lucy heads over to

Luciana's house, she's been helping her study for her GED. She'll be taking it in two months. Lucy's so excited and she says after she's done, she wants to be a veterinarian. Maeve Bastianini, Franco's wife, is studying to be one. She's specializing in exotic animals, specifically sea otters. Lucy says she wants to choose to specialize in another animal. Maybe horses or another exotic animal. I'm so proud of her.

As we make the turn onto Main Street in downtown Lake Renegade, my body freezes. I swear I just saw my parents. They were sitting in the gazebo. But it can't be, right? There's no way they could find us. My hand instinctively goes to my belly to protect it.

"Are you okay, Simone?" Raziel asks.

I know I shouldn't keep this from him, but I don't want him to think I'm crazy.

"Yeah, everything's fine," I answer with a smile.

I glance back over to the gazebo and no one's there. I must be going crazy.

When we get to the bakery, I help put out the freshly baked pastries that we sell. Some days I come in early to help bake, and some days I start later. We open at seven in the morning and close up at six o'clock in the evening. Unless we sell out. Then we get to go home early. That happens more often than I thought it would. We have people that will drive in from the neighboring counties just to get our pastries. This is definitely my dream job.

"Morning," I say to Rosaura, Gráinne and Caitríona.

They all come over and give me a hug. I've never hugged so much in my whole life. I can't say it's a bad feeling.

"How is baby doing?" Rosaura asks.

"Peanut is good. We're supposed to go to the doctor for our first ultrasound."

"Are you planning on finding out what you're having?" Gráinne asks.

"We haven't decided." I laugh. "We keep going back and forth. What do you think we should do?"

All of them smile at me.

"It depends. Sometimes it's nice to know. But on the other hand, having it be a surprise is fun too." Gráinne chuckles.

"Wow, I'm not sure you're helping." Caitríona laughs.

"Hey, I tried." Gráinne makes faces at her.

We spend the next hour getting things ready so we can open. It's always a comfortable silence in the bakery when we're doing this. When I was with my parents, silence wasn't comfortable. Usually silence led to yelling and then hitting. It took me a while to not jump at every noise.

Our day goes smoothly, just like most of our days.

"I have to head out to my appointment."

"Is Romano coming here to get you?" Rosaura asks.

"No, he's meeting me there."

"Okay. Be safe."

I turn to Raziel and he opens the door for me.

"Thank you." I smile as we head out. It's a ten minute walk, but it's a nice one. Lake Renegade is a really great town, I've also talked to people who want to stay here. So they end up renting a house or apartment and find jobs. I hear their stories sometimes while they sit and eat our pastries.

"We found you! Are you okay? Were you kidnapped?"

I hear a voice yelling, I turn and see my parents. How did they find us? Raziel steps in front of me and shields me from them.

"Who the fuck are you?" He growls at them.

"We're her parents, we thought we lost her. But here she is! Who are you? Are you the one that found our baby?" my father says.

How can they act like they're so concerned about me? I try to stay hidden behind Raziel, which is easy because he's a big guy. Not as big as my Romano, but still big. Speaking of my Romano, he's charging towards us.

"Who the fuck are you and why are you talking to my woman?" he asks, getting in my father's face.

"Your woman? What are you talking about? She's a child."

"I'm not a child. I'm twenty-one years old. And I wasn't kidnapped," I say from behind my Romano/Raziel wall.

"If you weren't kidnapped, what happened? We've given you everything and where is Lucy? She's not eighteen yet and that's kidnapping."

Now we're getting somewhere. This is the real them, they don't care, they just want control.

"It's none of your business where Lucy is," Romano says.

"It definitely is my damn business. She's my daughter and you're the criminal that took my children!" my father raises his voice at Romano.

Both Romano and Raziel step towards my father and he visibly cowers. I try to hold back a snicker but it slips out.

"You ungrateful little witch. We've done everything for you and this is how you repay us?" my mother snaps at me.

This is the first time I've ever heard her raise

her voice or call me names. I step around Romano and face her and my father.

"You don't scare me anymore. You can't hurt me anymore. And I promise you, you will never hurt Lucy again."

Before I can step back, my father reaches out and slaps me. Romano punches him before I can even react to it.

"Don't you ever touch my wife again."

"Your wife? What the hell are you talking about? You can't be married to her! She's an idiot with no education. And she hasn't been gone long enough for you to have married her!"

Romano looks like he's getting bigger with each word my father says against me. He slams my father against the wall.

"I will only say this once more. *Never* speak that way about my wife. In fact, don't ever speak to her again."

While Romano is talking to my father, my mother is calling the police. I hate her. It takes five minutes for the police to show up. Luckily it's Salvatore Mancini, Leonardo and Rosaura's oldest son and his partner, Mac Walker. They are detectives with the Chicago Police, and they also volunteer out here in our town.

"We heard the call over the radio. What's going on?" Salvatore asks.

"These two animals attacked us out of nowhere. We were minding our own business and they took our daughter." My mother starts to sob.

What the heck is going on? Why is she lying like that? Does she really think I would back her up? Salvatore looks at me, he knows what I've been through so I'm not worried. But Romano did assault my father. My mother looks me over.

"Oh my goodness, you're a whore!" she exclaims as she stares at my belly. In the last week, I've started to pop out a little, I love how Romano talks to our baby. But hearing my mother call me a whore? That takes me back to living with them and being ashamed and scared of everything I do.

Romano

"Let him go, Romano. We got this. Go to Simone, I think she needs you," Mac says to me.

Right as he says that, I hear Simone's mother call her a whore. And all I see is red. Blood fucking red. I would never hit a woman, but no one calls my wife a whore. I don't care who the fuck it is.

And I care even less that it's the bitch that tortured my woman.

I head over to Simone and wrap my arms around her.

"Are you okay, mia farfalla?"

"Are you calling her a whore in another language? Because if you are, I agree." Simone's father laughs.

"Shut it. Or I will let him loose on you," Mac says to him. "And you? Stop calling your daughter a whore."

Simone is shaking as I hold her. She's told me before about how her parents talked to her. But they were never really mean to Lucy, and I know it hurt her. But it was also a relief to her because she didn't want Lucy to go through that.

"M-maybe I should go with them. I don't want to bring this on you." She sniffles.

I tilt her chin to look up at me. "I love you. I'm not going to let you go. Not today, not tomorrow, not ever. And it's not because you're carrying our child. It's because I choose you. I'll always choose you."

I lean down and kiss her, holding her tight.

"I love you, Romano. I don't want to leave you. But if they try to take Lucy, I won't let her go alone," she says softly to me.

I understand what she's saying. But none of us will let them take Lucy either. As we stand here, more of my brothers and the Mancinis show up.

"Can you take Simone back to the bakery?" I ask Rosaura.

"Of course. Come on, sweet girl. You don't need this stress."

I watch them walk away, then turn to her parents.

"I don't know you, and from what I've heard? You don't deserve to be parents to anyone. So I'll say this once. Stay the fuck away from Simone and Lucy. I don't care what rights you think you have. But abusing your children is never an option."

Simone's father laughs. "Is that what she told you? That we abused them? We never put a hand on any of our kids."

What a fucking cocksucker, he really wants us to think that he's innocent in all of this? That he didn't terrorize his kids, making all four of them run from him? I want to put my fist through his smug face.

"I'm going to ask you and your wife to leave the area. Your daughter is an adult and it is her choice to talk to you or not," Salvatore says.

"You can't make us leave. This is a free

country," Simones father says. I still don't know the asswipe's name.

"Actually I can. I am the law here in Lake Renegade. And we don't allow people like you to ruin our town," Sal responds calmly.

Asswipe scoffs at him. "This town is a shit hole and it harbors criminals. I want my daughters back. I'll go to the real police and they'll help me get her back."

"Unfortunately sir, both your daughters have already made reports with the Chicago police. There is a restraining order in place and a court date scheduled. I'm guessing that's why you're here. Somehow you found out where they were. Which is illegal and I can arrest you for being anywhere near Simone."

Simone's father looks like he's going to explode which makes me want to laugh. He thought he could come here and just take Simone and Lucy away. He's going to learn that's not how things work here in Lake Renegade. Even if Simone wasn't my woman, we would still protect her and Lucy.

"Lucy is only seventeen years old. She's still a minor and you have no right to keep her from me. You can keep the pregnant whore."

What Simone's parents don't know is that Lucy

has been emancipated. It took three months to get all the papers together and we all testified for her. She got her final papers last week. She's officially free of them. I wish I could blurt that out to them, but it's not my news to tell.

I take a few steps towards Asswipe. I warned him that if he called my farfalla names again I would make him pay. He sees me coming and starts to back up. That coward is barely five-eight and at my full height? I have at least seven inches and one hundred pounds on him. I will kill the bastard.

"You can't touch me. I will press charges and you'll go to jail." His voice betrays his fear of me.

"He's not worth a night in jail, Romano," Sal says quietly to me. "Fuck him. He's lost everything, and we win. Don't let him take anything from you and Simone."

Salvatore is right. But that doesn't mean it's not killing me to walk away from the bastard. This isn't the end, I will get revenge for Simone.

Chapter Thirteen

Romano

It's been three days since Simone's parents confronted her outside the bakery. We never did make it to our appointment. And I've been worried about her stress levels. Lucy has been really quiet too. Salvatore has kept us in the loop, their parents have gone to the main police station in Chicago to try and get some help. But as of now, they've been told they need to wait. They have tried to get onto the property, but every person that takes care of the gates has been told not to let them in.

I hate that I won't be able to go with Simone to

the bakery today. Maeve has classes and this is my job, to protect her. But I know that Raziel will take care of her.

"How are things with Simone's parents?" Maeve asks me as we head to her first class.

"It's quiet which is never a good sign." I sigh.

She nods. "Especially in this family. Maybe they'll just leave?"

"I doubt it, but it would be the best case scenario."

Since this morning I've had a bad feeling about today. I hate days like this when I just can't put my finger on what might happen. I call Raziel to check in. I don't usually call Simone in case she's in the middle of making something.

"You miss your woman already?" He laughs as he answers.

"You're a dick, how are things?" I laugh.

"It's calm today, but I have a weird feeling. Like when Luciana was taken, weird feeling."

My body tenses up when he says that.

"I've been feeling like that all day too. It's her fucktard parents. They need to leave Lake Renegade, I don't even know why they're still here."

"But they've been laying low. You think they'd really start shit?" Raziel asks.

"I do. Her father is a coward. I think he'll try to take the girls because he thinks he can. But he won't do it right in front of us."

"Don't worry, I got your girl. I just hate this feeling. and it's not just me. Azrael, Arturo and Seamus are here too. So we have more than enough eyes in the bakery."

"I'll head over there when Maeve is done with classes. She was saying we need pastries."

Raziel chuckles. *"I'll make sure they save you some."*

"Thanks. Maeve has two more classes. So maybe a couple hours. Tell Simone if she sees them, she needs to let you know."

"Don't worry, brother. She knows."

When I hang up, I look around the campus. Next semester, Simone and Lucy will be attending Blue University. Lucy wants to follow Maeve and be a veterinarian. Simone was saying she might want to be a psychologist. After everything she's been through, she wants to help others who have been through it too. I love that about her. How no matter what she's gone through, she's still found a way to love unconditionally. She still wants to help others. I can't wait to see her as a mother.

I smile at Maeve as she comes out of class, one

of her classmates is whispering to her and giggling. I'm used to the stares I get from them.

"How was class?" I ask her.

"It was good, I can't wait to start my veterinarian classes. Also that girl? The one that was giggling? She likes you, she's been watching you all semester. I told her you're married and expecting, I'm pretty sure she's crushed now."

I chuckle. "Sorry."

"Don't be sorry, I love your story with Simone. It's a beautiful one, and one that your children and grandchildren will love."

"Sometimes I forget how all of you are such hopeless romantics," I tease her.

We get to her last class of the day when my phone rings.

____

Simone

____

I don't know what my parents are up to in Lake Renegade. From what Salvatore has told us, they're still here. I wish they would just leave. Lucy is scared and won't leave the property. But I refuse to let them win. So I go to work today, like every other day. We get the bakery ready and open. And like most days, we have a line waiting outside. It always makes me smile. Since my parents showed up, there are bodyguards watching each door. No one would be able to come in without them knowing.

The day goes by fast—we're busier than usual, which I like because it means I get to see Romano sooner. I head into the back of the bakery to grab more doughnuts to put out. Something catches my eye by the back door. When my eyes finally focus on it, I see my father standing there with a gun in his hand. Seamus is lying at his feet and I can see blood seeping from his chest.

"Get the fuck over here. And do it quietly," my father says to me.

I slowly make my way over to him, hoping that if I take a while, someone out front will notice. Because it doesn't take that long to get doughnuts. I say a silent prayer that Seamus is still alive. I try to see if he's breathing, but I can't tell. When I get close enough, my father grabs my arm and yanks me to him. I try to be quiet, because I know what will happen if I make noise. Would he shoot more people? And why didn't we hear the gun go off?

I wish Romano was here, his presence gives me strength. But at the same time, I'm glad he's not.

The crazy look in my father's eyes tells me that he would kill anyone who tries to help me.

"Why are you doing this?" I ask him.

"Shut your mouth. You're coming back with us and that bastard you're carrying will be sold."

Wait. He wants to sell my baby? Why?

"Please, just let me go. I won't tell anyone what you've done."

He raises his hand and slaps me across my face. I've learned not to cry out when he does this and my instincts kick in again. I need to protect my baby and find a way to get away from him. I let him pull me outside and into the car where my mother is waiting.

"We need to get Lucy," she says to my father.

I laugh. "You'll never get near Lucy."

My father points the gun at my belly. "That's why you'll call her and have her meet you somewhere."

"She's not stupid. She won't come and meet me, she knows you're here."

"Then you'll go there and take her out with you."

"You shot someone. Someone that my family will notice is missing."

"Your 'family'? You're dumber than I thought. They're not your damn family. They're using you to breed. And you're a whore so of course you went along with it."

From the moment we got into the car, I had my phone on. As my father was opening the back door to get me out of the bakery, I dialed Romano. I heard him answer. But when my father yelled at me, he went silent. So I know he's still listening. If there's one thing I'm one hundred percent sure of? It's that my Romano will never stop looking for me. And it's at this exact moment I realize that my parents are going to die. Even if they kill me first, they will die at the hands of my new family.

Romano

Every time I see Simone's name flash on my screen, I can't help the smile that spreads on my face.

"Farfalla," I say.

Then I hear her father tell her to shut her mouth. And that they plan to take our baby and sell it. That man will be dead soon. I put my phone on mute. Luckily, I see Maeve coming out of class at this exact moment. I hurry over to her.

"We need to leave," I say to her and lead her to the cage we rode in today.

"What's going on?" she asks. "Is Franco okay?"

Recently we had problems with a rival club and Franco was shot. So I understand her worrying about him.

"Franco is fine," I say as I put my phone down carefully in the car.

We hear Simone's mother talk about how they need to get Lucy. And how Simone will be the one to get her to come out. The whole conversation is making me more and more angry. Maeve gasps beside me.

"I need you to do me a favor. Call Raziel and find out where he is and how those bastards got my girl," I growl out. "Please."

Maeve nods and calls Raziel. She puts him on speaker phone.

"What do you mean 'where's Simone'?" Raziel sounds genuinely confused.

"She called me. I heard that bastard take her. She's in a car with them and they're talking about getting Lucy."

"Fuck! Give me a second. I need to go look, she just went to the back to get more doughnuts."

"Hurry!" I yell as he hangs up.

I need to get Maeve back to the property before

I can do anything. I would never forgive myself if something happened to her.

"Where are you going? The bakery is the other way." Maeve frowns at me.

"I need to get you home. I can't put you in any danger."

"No, I'm going with you. You need to find her now. If you take the time to drop me off, you could lose her forever. I'll call Franco and tell him what's going on. I know he'll meet us at the bakery."

She gets on the phone to Franco and I hear him say he'll meet us there, so I turn around. I just hope this isn't the wrong choice.

When we get to the bakery, several of my Cimaruta brothers are there, along with some of the Mancini family. We get out of the cage and Maeve heads straight to Franco.

"Do we know anything?" I ask anyone who's listening.

"I pulled the camera footage. Simone's father came up to the back door. I'm thinking Seamus didn't know it was him, he was wearing a baseball cap. Deliveries come around that time so it's not unusual for him to open it. As soon as Seamus opened the door, he shot him."

"Fuck. Is Seamus dead?"

"He's in surgery, the guys drove him to Lucciola Memorial. So we won't know for a while. And Sal is on his way," Franco explains.

"We also have the roads in and out of Lake Renegade closed. Let's hope they're still within our town limits," Giacomo says.

I hold my phone up and we can hear Simone's father screaming at her.

"I have it on mute. Simone called me and when I realized something was wrong, I put my end on mute."

"Good thinking," Sebastiano says. "Can I take your phone? I'll see if I can track where they are."

I nod and hand over my phone just as we hear a slapping sound. I'm going to kill him and then bring the bastard back just so I can kill him a second time.

There aren't many places he can go where we can't find them if he's still in our town. I go over to where Sebastiano has set up a little workstation.

"Has anything else happened?' I ask him as I sit down.

"No. The mother is calling her names and telling her that she'll never see the baby. But your woman is strong, Romano. She's holding her ground."

That's my woman, she's stronger than she thinks she is.

Chapter Fourteen

Simone

"Fuck!" my father yells as he sees a police checkpoint at one of the ways out of town. There are four ways in and out of town, and seeing this here? I'm betting that there's one at every one of them. Somehow I keep myself from laughing at this situation. My father is so angry that he has no idea where he's going. It looks like he's heading back towards the town square. I hope he is, because I know my family is there.

"You and Lucy are coming home with us. I don't care what you want. And I know you're not married to that criminal. We had the police check the records."

How is this even happening? I'm trying not to panic, I know this stress can't be good for Peanut. I rub my belly.

"I can't believe you let someone fuck you and now you're going to pay the price for spreading your legs," my father snaps at me.

I hate both of them. I've never used curse words, but he makes me want to start. Why couldn't they have left us alone? They don't love us and they never made us feel like they wanted us. I can see that he's heading towards the bakery. I don't think he knows this. As he gets closer, I can see a couple of police cars blocking the street that leads to the bakery. My father stops the car.

"Fine. If this is the way you want it? This is how it's going to end. Your criminal is going to watch you and that bastard child die."

He can't be serious, right? My father has hit me and screamed at me. But kill me? That thought never crossed my mind. My father gets out of the car and my mother follows him. There are guns pointed at them as he comes to my door and yanks me out. I hit my belly on the door as he does and I cry out at the pain that shoots through my belly.

"I'll trade you," my father yells at the police.

"This whore for the criminal that put this bastard child in her."

I watch Romano step forward without any hesitation.

'NO!" I start sobbing as he comes forward. I can't watch him die.

My father starts laughing as he watches Romano come forward and my reaction to it.

Romano

When that asshole pushes Simone around and says me for her? I don't even hesitate. I know for a fact that if I die today, my woman and my baby will be taken care of. I will make sure her father dies first. I haven't pulled my gun out yet. I walk towards them as Simone is sobbing and saying no. Her father is laughing at her pain and that fuels my anger even more.

"I'm here. Let Simone go," I say to him.

Her father laughs more and throws her to the ground. Simone lands on her belly, and her mother puts a foot on her back. She's going to die today too, maybe not by my hand. But she will join her husband in hell.

"You said me for her. Are you too much of a fucking coward to hold to your own deal?"

"Fuck you. You don't make the rules here, I do. And she doesn't deserve to live."

"I think you have that backwards, you're the one who shouldn't be alive."

Her father laughs. "You think you're going to kill me? I have all these witnesses that will say that you are the one who deserves to die with this bitch."

Okay, I've had enough of this bullshit. He hasn't lowered his gun so I pull mine out. Before I can point it at him, he takes a shot at me. On top of being a total assfuck, he can't hit what's right in front of him. And I'm a big fucking target. I point my gun at him. I hear the police cocking their guns behind me. It's Salvatore and his partner Mac. Salvatore understands why this has to be me. And I know that since her father has taken a shot at me, this becomes self-defense.

"Don't take another step closer!" he yells at me as he points the gun at Simone.

I can't wait any longer, I aim at her father and pull the trigger. The first hits him in the shoulder, I'm hoping that will make him back up and stop. I step towards them and he raises his gun at me again. This time he clips my arm and I hear Simone scream. Before I can raise my gun again, a shot rings out from behind me. I watch Simone's father fall, the gun in his hand slides over to her mother. She picks it up and looks at me.

"Fine. You win. You and this whore," she says as she raises the gun and shoots herself in the head.

I rush over to Simone and help her up, while Salvatore and Mac check her father and mother just to be sure. I pick her up and carry her to the cage where Raziel is waiting. Everyone is silent as we head to Lucciola Memorial Hospital. I'm so worried about her and our Peanut. And Simone is sobbing in my arms while she holds onto her tiny belly.

Simone

I keep repeating in my head over and over. *Please let peanut be okay.*

When we get to the hospital, they get me on a gurney and whisk me away. I hear myself screaming for Romano and finally they allow him to come with me.

"I'm here, mia farfalla. It's okay."

I feel my nerves start to calm down when I hear

his voice. But then, there's a cramping sensation in my belly and I wince.

"We need to get an ultrasound and figure out what's going on," the doctor says. "I think the stress and trauma is putting her into early labor."

"Can you stop it?" Romano asks. "It's way too early for the baby."

"We're going to do everything we can. Let's get her the ultrasound first."

I look at Romano and for the first time since I met him, he looks scared. And if he's scared? This has to be worse than I'm thinking it is.

"Peanut has to be okay," I say to him.

"Don't worry, Simone. We're going to get through this. It's just a bump in the road of our life," he says as he kisses me.

I hope he's right. I don't know if I could survive losing Peanut. And I don't know if Romano could go through it again.

The next sound we hear is a fast thumping sound.

"Is that Peanut?" I look at the doctor.

He nods at me. "That's your baby. The heartbeat is strong. Now we need to stop the contractions you're having."

We spend the next few hours waiting to see if the medicine they're giving me works.

"What if they can't stop it?" I whisper to Romano.

"They will. Our Peanut is strong and we're going to meet him or her in six months."

A nurse comes in to check on me. "Do you want to find out the sex of your baby?"

Romano and I look at each other and say 'no thank you' at the same time. I love him so much.

Chapter Fifteen

Simone

Today we're celebrating our one year anniversary of being in Lake Renegade. My parents died eight months ago. I wish I could say that I missed them. But it was because of them that I almost lost my baby. Because of them, I was put on bed rest for my entire pregnancy. The only time I was allowed out of it was when I married my soulmate. The man that made every dream that I never knew I wanted come true.

Somehow Salvatore took care of the whole situation with my parents. There were enough bystanders to testify that my father attacked me and then Romano. And Romano acted in self-defense. Then my mother took the gun that my father had and shot herself. I never got to ask them why they raised us the way they did. Why they never loved us. I've slowly come to terms with all of it. There's nothing else I can do, I'll never know why. But I do know that I want to go to college and get my psychology degree so that I can help others who've had to go through what we all did.

Romano gave me a family. Lucy and I are safe and loved. Something we've never had till now. The greatest gift that he gave me was our daughter. Giulietta Lucy Vietti was born one-and-a-half months early. But now she's a perfectly healthy six-month-old baby. A few weeks before she was born, Romano and I had a simple ceremony in my hospital room. Raziel married us, just like he marries everyone else in our family. It was perfect. Romano says he wants to give me the big wedding we talked about before. But I don't think I need that anymore. I have everything I could ever want already.

The only real thing that's missing is Thomas and Robin. So far we haven't been able to find them and it makes me sad. I miss them so much. Romano says that Sebastiano and Francesco, who are the best with computers, will never stop looking. I will always hold out hope that we will find them.

Romano

When I first lost Amara and our children, I thought that if I moved on and had another family, it would be a betrayal to them. But I've come to realize that it's not. I feel it deep in me that they're happy for me. That this is what Amara would've wanted for me. Finding Simone healed me in so many ways.

After I shot her father, I worried that it could change how she felt about me. Even thought I wasn't the one that ended his life, I worried that she might have some sort of resentment towards me for doing it. But she's had none of that, we've talked a lot about it. And she knows that his death was the only way that he would leave her and Lucy alone. I just wish I could've made him suffer for all the pain he put Simone through. He made her entire life a living hell. Even though the abuse didn't start when they were children, it still evolved to that. No man should ever put their hands on a woman. Especially not your own daughter.

When Giulietta was born, I've never been more terrified in my life. She was a preemie and we were told that they couldn't give us a one-hundred-percent yes that she would survive. I learned that my daughter is a fighter like her mamma. Within a week she was breastfeeding and home a month after she came into this world.

I have one more surprise for mia farfalla. It's been a hard one to keep quiet. But it's going to be worth it.

Today we're celebrating Simone and Lucy being with us for a year. We all turn to the stage as Caitríona stands up there.

"Hey, everyone. Okay, we all know what we're here for. To celebrate Simone and Lucy. They've been through so much and come out stronger. We all love you both so much. All of us here have a surprise for the two of you. I need you both up here with me," Caitríona says.

I take Giulietta from Simone and give her a kiss. She and Lucy look a little nervous and I love it. When they get on stage, they're made to face one way and told they can't move. They're both laughing as they stand there.

"Okay. I think we're ready. Simone and Lucy? Turn around," Caitríona says.

I watch my wife and sister-in-law turn. Lucy

screams and launches herself at Thomas. Simone drops to her knees sobbing. Robin goes over to her and embraces her. Everyone is cheering and there's not one dry eye here.

Simone comes over to me and leads me over to Thomas and Robin. I've already met them, they've been here for a day now. Thomas shakes my hand and then gives me a hug. Robin is next. I hug them both.

"Thank you for bringing us back together," Thomas says. "I don't know how you did it, but thank you."

"It's not me you need to thank. Sebastiano and Francesco are the ones that found you two."

"But they said you were the one that set this in motion and you didn't give up looking for us." Robin smiles.

"I knew that this was the one thing I wanted to give to my wife," I say as I kiss Simone.

"I also wanted to thank you for everything you've done for my sisters. When I left them, it almost killed me. I almost went back for them. But I knew I couldn't support all four of us just yet. I needed to get a job and a home. Then I planned on going back for Simone and Lucy."

"I know you did your best. That's what they both told me. Now that all of you are safe, if you and Robin want to stay in Lake Renegade, I'm sure we can find jobs you'll like and we definitely have a home for you."

"I don't know what we did to deserve all of this. But know that I appreciate it," Thomas says as he wipes tears from his eyes.

"We're family here. You're family now. We got your back," I say to them.

Baby Breeder Session 2

Ready for the next book in the Baby Breeder
Session 2 series?

Bred by the Mercenary by Amanda Keen <u>mybook.</u>
<u>to/BredbytheMercenary</u>

BABY BREEDER SESSION 2 SERIES

What better way to ring in the New Year than with babies?

This January, join some of your favorite romance authors as they bring you Baby Breeder Session 2, a series all about making babies. Whether it's a primal, biological need or something else driving these men to breed the women they love, what is guaranteed is these stories are going to be hot and messy. Every happily ever after doesn't have to have babies, but these men want nothing less than their women round and glowing.

Check out the special deliveries from the Baby Breeder Session 2 Series!
mybook.to/BabyBreederSession2

Rough Riding by Ember Davis mybook.to/RoughRiding

Bred by the Villain by Penelope Wylde mybook.to/BredbytheVillain

Breeding the Nanny by Darcy Rose mybook.to/BreedingtheNanny.

Bred by the Cowboy by Krista Ames mybook.to/
BredbytheCowboy

Moore Than Expected by Mayra Statham mybook.
to/MooreThanExpected

Bred by the Enemy by Jessa Joy mybook.to/
bredbytheenemy

Artfully Bred by E.M. Shue mybook.to/
ArtfullyBred

Bedded and Bred by Tamrin Banks mybook.to/
BeddedandBred

Bred to the Mafia Beast by Layne Daniels mybook.
to/BredtotheMafiaBeast

Bred by the Boss by Cassi Hart mybook.to/
BredbytheBoss

Bred by Daddy by Stella Bella mybook.to/
BredbyDaddy

Stalked & Bred by Tracie Douglas mybook.to/
Stalked-Bred

Bread in The Oven by Natalie Arthur <u>mybook.to/</u> <u>BreadinTheOven</u>

Bred by the Mercenary by Amanda Keen <u>mybook.</u> <u>to/BredbytheMercenary</u>

Bred by the Deputy by Dee Ellis
Sweet Child of Mine by Euryia Larsen <u>mybook.</u> <u>to/SweetChildofMine</u>

Ravaged & Bred by KL Donn <u>mybook.to/Ravaged-</u> <u>Bred</u>

After the Final by Katharine O'Neill <u>mybook.to/</u> <u>AftertheFinal</u>

About the Author

Hi! I'm Natalie. I published my first book, Aftermath in August 2021. I've been lucky enough to find my own insta-love-at-first-sight person. We have a daughter who drives us crazy and a corgi who adds to the chaos. I love hockey (Chicago Blackhawks), MotoGP (Motorcycle Racing), and baseball (Chicago Cubs). When I'm not writing, you can find me studying or crafting. Or crafting when I should be studying.

Nataliearthurbooks.com

<u>Giovanna</u>

Everything I thought about my life was a lie and because of that, trust became non-existent for me. Then I met Declan. He pushed his way into my life, determined to prove to me that not everyone is a liar. He's a hockey player and we all know the reputation of hockey players. But I want to trust someone again…maybe he's the one?

<u>Declan</u>

Hockey has been my focus for as long as I can remember. The day I met Giovanna, my life changed. Hockey would always be my first love. But she would be my last. Something happened to her and she's afraid to trust me. But that's okay, I'll show her that I'm real. That we're real.

Aftermath is the first book in my Mancini Legacy Series. All books are standalone, but it's best if read in order. There is mention of characters from my Cimaruta MC Chicago Series.

https://books2read.com/Aftermath-ManciniLegacy-BookOne

<u>Sebastiano</u>

I had given up on meeting my person, content to be the protector of my family. Then one day I met her. But someone else was laying claim to her. If she was happy, I would step back and watch her from afar. But then I saw the marks on her and I knew I needed to save her.

<u>Schuyler</u>

It seems like I've been struggling most of my life. Just my

sister and me against the world. Then I thought I met the man of my dreams. Turns out he's the man from my nightmares. I can't run and I can't escape from him. Then I met Sebastiano. He made me feel safe from the moment he took my hand in his. He says I will be his, but he doesn't know about the monster that's in my life. The one that won't let go.

Saving Her is the second book in my Mancini Legacy Series. All books are standalone, but it's best if read in order. There is mention of characters from my Cimaruta MC Chicago Series.

https://books2read.com/SavingHer-ManciniLegacy-BookTwo

<u>Luciana</u>

Women on an MC council? It's unheard of until now. Love at first sight? That's a new one for me too. I was convinced I didn't need someone to make me happy.

Then I slammed into Rónán.

Literally.

In an instant, he turned my world upside down. But can he handle the MC life?

<u>**Rónán**</u>

My life was going the way I planned it. Then the most beautiful woman stepped into my path and changed my life forever. I know she's keeping things from me. And that's okay...for now.

Because she's mine.

She just doesn't know it yet.

Choices is the first book in my Cimaruta MC Chicago Series. All books are standalone, but it's best if read in order. There is mention of characters from my Mancini Legacy Series.

https://books2read.com/Choices-CimarutaMC-BookOne

Francesco

I met the love of my life at fourteen. She had my heart the moment I saw her. But when you're young and stupid you don't always make the right decisions. That's what happened to me. I let the temptations of my job distract me from the one thing I couldn't live without. I had lost all hope, but fate gave me another chance. I have to make it up to her. I know she's hiding something from me. Will she let me in and give me a second chance?

<u>**Maeve**</u>

I thought I had it all. Sure I may have been young, but when it's real, you just know. That was, until he ended things. I never saw it coming. Now he's back and he wants another chance. Can I really trust him not to break my heart again? I want to believe him. I've never stopped loving him. But it's not just me I have to protect anymore.

Can they find their way back to the happily ever after they were meant to have? Or will they be pulled apart again, shattering all hope?

Reclaiming Our Forever is the second book in my Cimaruta MC Chicago Series. All books are standalone, but it's best if read in order. There is mention of characters from my Mancini Legacy Series.

https://books2read.com/ReclaimingOurForever-CimarutaMC-BookTwo

<u>Amante</u>

Relationship? No.

Love? Hell no.

Forever? Never.

A quick hook up and that was that. I had my family and my club and that's all I needed. Until the day she walked in. With her I wanted more than one night, but when I

got out of the shower she was gone. But I will find her.
Then I'll just have to convince her we belong together.

<u>Charmaine</u>

Love is nothing but a lie. I watched my parents crash and
burn and nothing and no one could change my mind.
Until him. My tattooed, hunky biker man. Wait, did I say
mine? That can't happen. But he says all the right things,
and makes me feel like I'm the most special girl in the
world. Can we make it work?

**Notch the Plan is part of the Notchin' Boots
Series. There is mention of characters from
my Mancini Legacy Series and my Cimaruta
MC Chicago Series.**

https://books2read.com/NotchThePlan-
NotchinBootsSeries

<u>Hollis</u>

The people you're born to don't always turn out to be your 'family'. Families can be chosen, and I chose the Cimaruta MC. They've been there with me for the last six years, and I thought I had everything I needed. One night was all it took to make me want more. But she's hiding something from me and I need to know what it is. I will save her from anything. That much I do know.

<u>Lila</u>

My life was finally going smoothly. It was me and my daughter against the world. I worked at a club called Club Curve—I'm a curvy girl, so why not? Then one night, HE walked in. Now he's turning my life upside down and I'm not sure how to feel about it. My biggest fear is about to become a reality.

Just as you are is a stand alone and part of the Club Curve series. But there is mention of characters from my Mancini Legacy and Cimaruta MC Chicago series.

https://books2read.com/JustAsYouAre-ClubCurveSeries

<u>Kostas</u>

Mating matches keep the peace in our world. So why did it feel like my life was over when it was my turn? She hated me from the moment we were paired. And to be honest? I hated her too. So when she rejected me for some loser from another clan, it didn't bother me that much. But then I met her—the one the fates chose for me —and everything just felt right. I knew in an instant that she was the one I would never let go of.

<u>Artemis</u>

In our world, mates can be either fated or chosen, but finding your fated mate is never guaranteed. I thought I had chosen someone who could love me and we would spend our lives together. But then he rejected me—for my BEST FRIEND. That day, I decided I was fine being alone. But then, completely by chance, I met someone who felt like home. Could this really be it? The forever I secretly craved...my fated one.

My Fated One is part of the Fated Mates Series. There is mention of characters from my Mancini Legacy Series and my Cimaruta MC Chicago Series.

https://books2read.com/MyFatedOne-FightingFateSeries

Aiden

Motorcycle racing has been my life since I could walk and talk. It was all I ever needed. Or so I thought. Then I met the one woman that made me want more. One day, the unthinkable happens—a racing accident causes me to lose all my memories of her. But I still feel her in my soul, even if my brain can't remember her.

Élodie

I wanted a knight in shining armor, but what I got was a wolf in disguise. After escaping from him, I met a man willing to give me everything I ever wanted. Then in a split second, he was taken from me. Not physically, but mentally. The man I love doesn't remember who I am, but I'm determined to get him back.

Racing Back to Love is part of the Forget-Me-Not Series. There is mention of characters from my Mancini Legacy Series.

https://books2read.com/RacingBackToLove-ForgetMeNotSeries

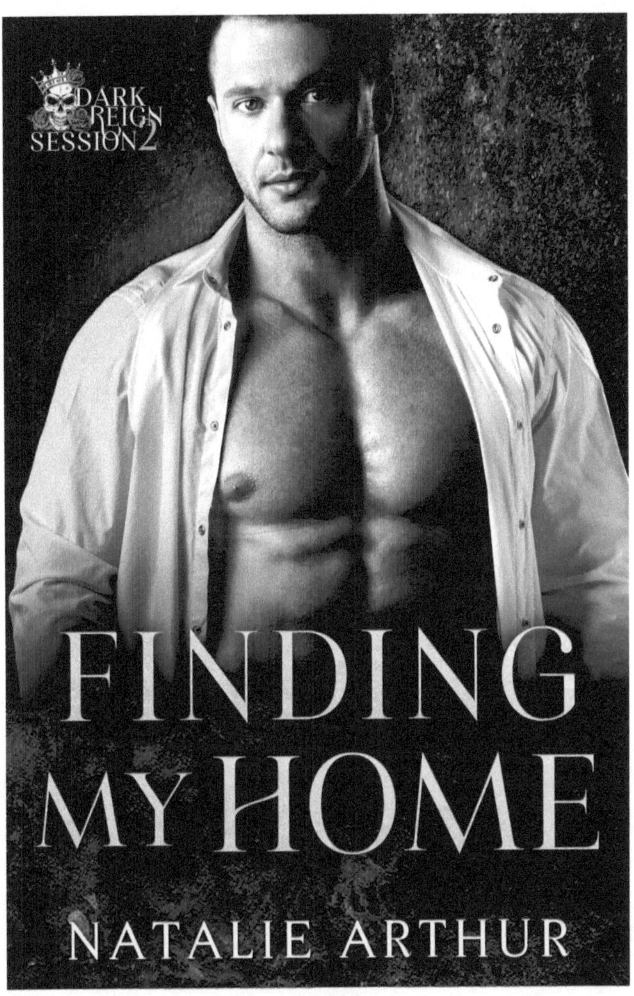

<u>Niccolò</u>

My first real memory is watching my papà gunned down in front of me. I was only five years old. I've spent my life waiting for things to fall into place, and now we have the means to avenge him. But the woman I love is caught in the middle. I have to keep her safe, but I can't just walk away. I need this too.

<u>Mirabelle</u>

When I was two, my father killed my mother and then himself. Luckily, I don't remember that at all. My sister raised me the best she could and made sure we stayed together. I have finally met the man of my dreams, but being with him means dealing with things I don't understand. Will he find a way to protect me or will he be too late?

Finding My Home is part of the Dark Reign Sessions 2 Series. There is mention of characters from my Mancini Legacy Series and Cimaruta MC

https://books2read.com/RacingBackToLove-ForgetMeNotSeries

www.ingramcontent.com/pod-product-compliance
Lightning Source LLC
Chambersburg PA
CBHW061535310726
48972CB00008B/2461